A DOG'S LIFE

MICHAEL HOLROYD

MACLEHOSE PRESS
QUERCUS · LONDON

First published in the USA in 1969 by Holt, Rinehart and Winston
First published in Great Britain in 2014 by

MacLehose Press
an imprint of Quercus
55 Baker Street
7th Floor, South Block
London W1U 8EW

A CIP catalogue record for this book is available
from the British Library.

ISBN (HB) 978 1 84866 522 4
ISBN (Ebook) 978 1 84866 523 1

This book is a work of fiction. Any resemblance to
living persons is entirely coincidental.

10 9 8 7 6 5 4 3 2 1

Designed and typeset in Albertina by Libanus Press Ltd., Marlborough
Printed and bound in Great Britain by Clays Ltd, St Ives plc

CONTENTS

A lost thing could I never find
    Nor a broken thing mend:
And I fear I shall be all alone
    When I get towards the end.
Who will there be to comfort me
    Or who will be my friend?

HILAIRE BELLOC, "The South Country"

A DOG'S LIFE

Chapter 1

NIGHT

Three o'clock struck from the old church tower at the end of the garden. The notes, long and mournful in the cool night air, trembled among the leaves of the trees, echoed faintly through the dark flower beds and across the shadowy lawn to the house. Inside This'll Do the Farquhar family, all but two, slept in the separate bedrooms that led off from a circular landing on the first floor.

Eustace Farquhar, eighty years old and head of the family, lay stiffly on his back, his arms akimbo, in a few short hours of shallow and dreamless oblivion. His sunken mouth was open to the ceiling, and he breathed quickly, inaudibly. In a glass of water by his bedside, false teeth rested in silence. His supports coiled snakelike around his dressing table; over the arm of a chair lay bandages; spread out in two small heaps on the floor were his clothes and bedclothes.

In the room next door lay his wife Anne, tossing and turning under an untidy mountain of crumpled sheets, bottles, blankets, quilts and eiderdown. Every now and then a low moan, like a siren, came from her lips, the mountain erupted in the darkness, subsided, and all was silence again.

Miss Tooth, the antiquated nurse who had come some fifty years ago to help with the child, Henry, and stayed on to lend a hand, lay in the large converted cupboard next to her mortal enemy Anne, as infuriatingly still and noiseless in her sleep as in her waking life.

Nearby, in his bedroom on the other side of the landing, Henry Farquhar was trumpeting out loud and vigorous snores that shook and rattled the foundations of his bedstead. Through his head there rushed visions of fantastic cricket matches – white-flannelled figures on a pitch of glorious green all watching him, Henry Farquhar, amassing extraordinary scores.

His son, Kenneth, who had barely laid down *Grenades* and switched off the light, was sliding into unconsciousness, grateful to be set free, if only for an hour or two, from the ordeal awaiting him later that day.

But the neighbouring room, which belonged to his great-aunt Mathilda, was empty, the curtains billowing in before the night air from the open windows.

The three notes died and the house was left in quiet. A few minutes passed and then, Anne Farquhar opened her eyes.

Chapter 2

ALARUMS AND EXCURSIONS

No it had not been her imagination. Some *movement* downstairs had awakened her. She lay quietly listening in her bed. Earlier that night it had been raining cats and dogs, but now the sky outside was clearing and everything was still.

There it was again! *Noises* in the house. Cautiously she groped across and began fumbling with her clock. Half past three. *Distinct noises* from below – what could they mean? *Creakings* and *sounds* in the darkness. This time they were nearer and they seemed to come from the staircase. Were these the cut-throats and burglars for whom she had been waiting so long? Strange, having known for certain she would be murdered in her bed one of these fine days, that now it had come as such a shock. Her heart began palpitating violently.

She would have to raise the alarm and see them off. She felt for her emergency whistle, the whistle she used when she was ill – which she so often was these days. Her hand moved with exaggerated slowness so as to avoid disturbing them. She searched the table once, then again and finally a third time. Eustace's police whistle was not there. A bottle crashed to the floor. The night light on her chest of drawers bubbled erratically and in the leaping shadows she saw there was no whistle on the table. It must have rolled somewhere – and left her defenceless.

She took a deep breath, held it, and began struggling free from the vast bulk of her bedclothes. Once on her feet she crammed on a feather hat and her dressing gown and, clasping a flashlight in both hands, crept across to the door. Once there, bending almost double, she stopped to listen again – and heard a *distinct footstep* on the landing.

The crisis had come. As she stood here, this bent and fragile old woman, bravely pessimistic in her dressing gown, her slippers, her trembling hat, an ear pressed to a crack in the door, she tried to offer up a prayer to the Good Lord above and His Company of Saints. But the words did not offer themselves. She had forgotten them (she would be forgetting her own name next). The shock was too great. What could she be expected to do against those frightful clubs and daggers she was always reading about? Perhaps it was a nightmare. Perhaps she would wake suddenly to the sound of birds, the light of the morning sun. The illusion passed and with a sigh she lowered herself further down, squatting on her knees and peering through the keyhole to see how many of them there were and what they were up to.

From this position she could make out the silhouette of one of them, a rough brute standing motionless at the top of the stairs, his hand pressed to his forehead in thought. The figure turned and faced her door. She recoiled. It was her sister-in-law Mathilda! Flabbergasted, Anne opened the door and confronted her with the blinking torch.

"What's wrong, Mathilda?"

Mathilda stepped back from the blinding light that Anne was directing on and off into her face.

"Quiet!" she hissed.

At the fierce intensity of this command, Anne's trepidation rose once more. "How many of them are there?" she whispered.

"Are you perfectly potty?" Mathilda enquired. "Are you insane? For heaven's sake go back to bed!"

"But what, in the Lord's name, set you off gallivanting about the house at this unholy hour of the night?"

"Smith has vomited. Smith has brought up his pie. That's all. Now are you satisfied?"

"Too much meat, that's his trouble. Too much meat and pastry."

The two women stood facing each other, white with anger.

"Please go back to your bed this instant. And be so good as to remove that hat before you frighten someone."

"And you without a wink of sleep for weeks now, poor girl," sighed Anne.

"Bed!"

"Alright. Alright. I'll go." And with a snap Anne switched off her torch and the landing was stricken with darkness.

Chapter 3

NIGHT THOUGHTS

Back in her bedroom Mathilda gave herself up to worrying.

Something would have to be done. What it was she did not know, but for weeks now Smith had been getting worse. His present condition frightened her. Having made him as comfy as she knew how, she had finally reached her wits' end. Thinking of him lying downstairs, she could still see his large brown eyes rolling up at her, still hear the feeble thump of his rope-like tail, the gasping uneven breath.

No wonder she was worried. But her brother Eustace would never let her call in a vet. Not that he was a mean man. On the contrary, he was one of the kindest, most generous creatures in the world. But he had to be handled. Vets, he believed, belonged to the same breed of men as doctors – and his objections to doctors were many. Good health, in his view, could not be purchased or ladled out indiscriminately through a National Health Service. What was everyone's business, he said, was no-one's business. Mathilda shared his mistrust – anyway she would have felt it disloyal not to. Yet she could not blind herself to the fact that her brother's special cures and remedies, his syrups and concoctions, had not helped Smith.

Therefore something had to be done.

Meanwhile she was worried lest Anne, left standing outside on the landing, should wake everyone up. But there was nothing she could do. She stalked across to her cold hard bed, lay down abruptly, like some tin soldier suddenly knocked over, and continued to worry, frowning and open-eyed.

She was a practised worrier, Mathilda. She worried about Eustace who was over twenty years older than she was and needed all the sleep he could get at night; she worried about Miss Tooth for whom nothing was too good; she worried about her nephew Henry and his precious son Kenneth, both of whom were sure to resent being awakened on account of a mere dog. But most of all she worried about Anne, who was mad. She had never been too strong in the head, Anne. Had it not been for Miss Tooth, God knows what would have happened to the family. Anne had been too fond of her bridge to take care of anyone. Now that her partners were all dead, or as good as dead, and the velvet tables exiled to the garage, the wicked packs of cards all given to the hospital, she was thrown back on herself and had gone rapidly to seed. It was a worry. Perhaps they should consider a Home for her. The last thing they wanted was a raving lunatic on their hands – Smith was enough strain as it was.

Both problems, Smith and Anne, pointed to the same conclusion: *something would have to be done.*

The night wind tugged and fretted at her curtains, but Mathilda took no notice. And it was not until the church clock outside struck half past four that she lapsed uneasily into sleep.

Chapter 4

FRENCH WITHOUT TEARS

As the darkness outside began to lighten, the room to become alive with cool grey shapes and shadows, Anne was all at once startled by the shrilling of her alarm. Six o'clock. The dull beginnings of another dawn were already low in the sky, throwing a dim iridescence about her bedroom. Another day already. It was too soon. For although each heavy second lasted an eternity for Anne, the weeks and months and years spun past her with such effortless ease that she could recall her childhood as if it had all been packed into the previous day, and although she was always reminding others of her advanced age, she could never quite believe in it herself.

Where had the time gone? The long decades seemed to have shrivelled into a week or two. Only the other day she had been newly married – married at eighteen, and Eustace only three years older. Incredible! At times the conviction that she had never been young and happy would sweep over her. Then suddenly she would awake from such meandering visions to find herself buried in the unrelieved blankness of old age. How would it end? When would it end?

Now it was almost half past six and another breakfast was approaching. Would it never finish, this awful succession of meals, housework and more meals? She prayed not.

An hour later she had washed, dressed and stolen cautiously down the stairs on her way to "beginning the hall".

"Is everyone still alive?" Mrs Gaff, the cook, bustling in through the scullery, called out with macabre cheeriness. No-one answered – no-one ever answered. Half alive they were, half alive, half dead.

Anne left off "doing the mantelpiece" in the hall and hobbled along into the kitchen. When the cook had taken off her coat and energetically polished her hands, the two women settled themselves warmly in front of the huge stove and began to talk. The tea came to the boil and was poured out into yellow cups. They chatted on. Anne, with mournful euphoria, started her inventory of complaints: already the night was making her day. At least there was a bit of life about Mrs Gaff, she thought. Not like her own family.

Anne's conversation was a string of *non sequiturs* linked by a general sense of discontent. "I'm in the doghouse again," she confided. "But how was I to know? What with all these people in the house, it's no wonder burglars are attracted. And Smith's no use these days, not with all that meat inside him, all that meat and pastry. It's no joke by the time you're my age, Mrs

Gaff, as you'll soon be finding out – no joke at all. I wasn't brought up to it, you know. It was never like this in Canada."

She looked across at the cook sitting comfortably opposite her in a sagging canvas chair, and suddenly thought how lazy she was. Fat and lazy. If things had been left solely to her, the house would have gone to rack and ruin long ago. The stove rumbled and belched beside them like some prehistoric monster.

"You must have been a very wicked woman when you were young," Mrs Gaff giggled, pink in the face. "And now you're paying for it. Why don't you take up the football pools like me and win a fortune?"

Anne sighed hopelessly. "I can't fathom those pools," she declared. "They're too deep for me. I never could add two and two."

"Tell you what, then, if I go and win them this week, I'll give you each a thousand for keeps. Then all your troubles will be over and done with. How's that, then?"

"Go on with you, Mrs Gaff. What nonsense you talk." She was cheeky, of course, but Anne simply had to laugh. For she was a good soul, when all was said and done – though useless of course, quite useless.

"Well, I must be getting on with my work now," added the cook still chuckling. "Else you'll be giving me the sack, eh?"

Soon it was time for breakfast and Anne went to ask Mrs Gaff to blow the horn. They were a terrible family for meals.

Besides, Mrs Gaff enjoyed blowing the horn. Hurrying to the foot of the stairs, she let out three long and quivering blasts, each of them fit to wake the dead. There was an obscure sound from above, like a communal groan. Satisfied, she bustled back to the kitchen, beaming all over her face. "That should stir them up, madam," she cried. "I bet it shook up Mr Kenneth alright."

But all at once Anne looked grave. "It doesn't matter if *he* sleeps on. That blessed father of his keeps the child up all hours of the night what with lecturing him and so on. God knows what they find to talk about. Nobody tells me anything. I . . ."

But at that moment there sounded a roar from the hall. The door burst open and in strode Henry.

Chapter 5

THE LIFE AND HARD TIMES OF HENRY FARQUHAR

He was in a temper that morning. For several reasons – all of them good ones.

For the best part of his fifty years Henry had been the victim of bad luck. He'd had a particularly rotten start – dressed up like Little Lord Fauntleroy and paraded every bloody day before roomfuls of antique bridge-playing crones, so that his mother could show him off. His blood still ran cold when he remembered those afternoons. Then at school, he had just failed to get into the cricket team – a bitter disappointment that even now clouded his dreams.

Afterwards, in his early twenties, he had picked up a young redhead and been fool enough to marry her. She was a Swiss girl, easy enough to look at he would grant you, but quite impossible to manage, as he'd found out to his cost. They'd had a girl but she had gone and died on them in infancy. Then, not long after the birth of their only son, Kenneth, she packed her bags and left, simply ran off and no reason given. Henry had been as painstaking and long-suffering as he could be in his efforts to salvage the marriage, if only for the boy's sake. After all it would have cost her nothing to stay. But all she wanted was a good time for herself – and to hell with everyone else. Well, so far as Henry was concerned, it simply wasn't good enough. Of course she'd been bored with him – he knew that now: bored by his inability to behave like some idiot teenager; bored by his lack of ready cash; probably bored even by their child. She was a typically spoiled little bitch who needed to be put across someone's knee and given a good hiding – he sometimes wished he'd done that instead of trying to appeal to her better nature. She had no better nature. She simply traded on her good looks. Well, she'd find they wouldn't last for ever. Before she was very much older she would catch it in the neck – he was sure of that. After the divorce she'd gone and married one or two other luckless blokes, but of course no-one had been able to put up with her tantrums for long. Recently she'd got hitched up again to some fellow name of Stoat or Poach – poor blighter!

Still, at least she'd cured him of women. That was something to be said in her favour. You wouldn't catch him making that mistake again.

His business life had been unfortunate too. In the couple of jobs he'd had when younger, his exertions as advertising manager had resulted in a rapid build-up of orders that they could not meet and that made them bankrupt. If that wasn't bloody bad luck in life, he'd like to know what was.

Fact was, though, if only the old lady hadn't kicked up one hell of a shindy at the thought of her only son shaking the dust from his shoes and clearing out of the old country to join the family's corned beef set-up in northwest Canada, he'd be in clover today.

Ironically enough he'd done pretty well in the war. It was ironic because there was no future in the navy for a chap like him. Still, he'd knocked around a bit, seen what makes men tick, and finished up, to boot, as a captain. Not bad going.

Back in England he'd run into his very bloodiest patch of trouble. With only a hundred quid in his pocket and no time to lose, he'd moved like a blue-arsed fly to grab hold of whatever was going. Not that it amounted to much. All the best jobs had been snapped up by those buggers who'd shirked the fighting and stayed at home. It made one vomit. Some of the tasks he'd been obliged to buckle down to had been fucking awful, he didn't mind admitting. One couldn't have sunk much lower in life. On the other hand he bloody well couldn't afford to sit on his backside all day contemplating his navel. That would have driven him cuckoo in next to no time. Perhaps the younger generation had a thing or two to pick up from him in that respect – not that they ever would.

Anyway, at his age it had been no mean achievement to cotton on to this celluloid racket eighteen months back. There was a future in it he felt sure. Naturally, like every other job these days, the place was cluttered up with a pack of idiots. Take Belcher for instance (who was far too young for his position) and old Harris (who should have retired years ago). What a crew they were!

Some three years back he'd come to Cheshire to shack up at This'll Do with the rest of the family. Each morning he would drive twenty-five miles to his office outside Manchester; and each evening he drove back again. He enjoyed a good drive.

But life at This'll Do was beyond the pale. Just lately, with the animal a trifle out of sorts, it had been particularly hellish. You'd have thought the way they all went on that the end of the world was at hand. God's truth, if they had one quarter of his work on their plate, with all its problems and frustrations, they really would be in the soup.

Take that very morning for instance. To kick off with, at some unseemly hour of the night he'd been roused from his slumbers (just short of scoring his century!) by Mathilda padding around the house after the animal, and being further kept awake by the row that developed between her and the old lady just outside his bedroom door. This was an early start to the day even for such tried and hardy combatants as those two.

It was due to all this turmoil that he'd overslept – a most unusual performance for him. And this, of course, meant he'd have to face the ordeal of a communal breakfast. Normally, he hardly ate any breakfast and was well on his way to the office before the others had assembled. This saved the family both trouble and expense – though to hear the old lady carrying on, you'd never have guessed it. But he'd given up trying to please her these days. It simply wasn't worth the candle.

Now he was cornered without hope of escape, since he knew the old man would take it badly if he disappeared without going through the motions of breakfast. The old lady was sure to plague him about it – he knew her so well. He knew them all so well. They carried on like a lot of infants in swaddling clothes.

Henry was particularly infuriated at being late that day because at long last there seemed some chance that Belcher and old Harris had seen sense. For as long as he could remember he'd been begging them on bended knees to push ahead with the merger – and now it appeared as if they were actually listening to reason. And about ruddy time too. If he didn't force it through today, he'd eat his hat.

And as if all this was not enough for one mortal to put up with, he had no sooner descended the staircase than he heard the old lady maligning him in front of the cook. And about Kenneth too; Kenneth, who'd given him more headaches than all the rest of them put together. It was the bloody limit.

He stormed over to the kitchen and flung open the door.

Chapter 6

A MYSTERY

"Well speak of the devil!" cried Anne, throwing up her hands in alarm. "It's you Eustace – I mean Henry. What a turn you gave your poor old mother!"

"Nonsense!" shouted Henry, continuing his stride until he reached the refuse cans at the end of the scullery. "What unadulterated nonsense you do talk."

He turned on his heel and strode back like a Guardsman on parade.

"Don't believe a single word, will you, Mrs Gaff?" he called out. But already his anger had begun to ease. What was the point? It was hopeless lodging any protest.

Anne made a quick gesture to check her son's lack of taste. French was the proper language to use before servants and children on such occasions when you had something private to say, as Henry should have known. What, otherwise, had been the use of sending him to Repton?

Plain honest-to-God Anglo-Saxon was good enough for

him – always had been. He stood in the middle of the kitchen, his round red face one large frown, breathing fiercely, warming the room.

Anne wagged her finger. But the effect was less devastating than she intended, for at that moment Mrs Gaff waddled through to the scullery, her sleeves rolled up to reveal her thick orange arms.

"Well, I'm not sure what to believe," she let out. "Anyway, I 'spect Mr Kenneth is well able to take care of himself by now. If he's anything like my Jonathan . . ."

"I see you're down punctually for a change, Henry," interrupted Anne, saying the first thing that came into her head, for she knew that once Mrs Gaff started on about her Jonathan there was no telling how long they'd be there. But Henry (whom Anne sometimes thought an awful fool, even if he was her son) did not understand at all what she was on about. Instead he took his mother's utterance as being an allusion to his having overslept. He began walking up and down again.

"While we are on the subject of getting up," he retorted, "perhaps you would be good enough to inform me whether Kenneth has deigned to rise from his couch yet?"

"Oh do leave the boy alone for once in a while! He needs all the sleep he can get, poor mite."

By switching the subject to Kenneth, Henry had grasped the initiative. He was on familiar ground and could speak with authority.

"My dear mother," he explained, "he's been in bed a good five hours by my watch. You pamper the boy too much. I realise that as his mere father I am supposed to know less than nothing about such topics, but the plain truth of the matter is that all this mollycoddling will never stand him in good stead in life – mark my words!"

He came to a halt. Feet apart, hands on hips, he glared at Anne. She gave a faint moan. "Oh go to the dickens. I don't know what's got into you this morning. If you ask me, you got out of the wrong side of the bed."

"Well I know who is about to get out of his bed, one side or another, and that's Kenneth," replied Henry. And no amount of reasoning from Anne could prevent him from disturbing the boy. Henry could be very unreasonable at times, she thought, and as obstinate as a mule when he'd a mind to be. Where he got it from was a mystery.

Chapter 7

LOVE'S LABOUR'S LOST

They lay tightly in each other's arms upon the low couch. From the room beyond there floated the voluptuous chords, deep and slow, of a violin. Helen pressed forward, entwined her legs round his and rubbed herself against him like a cat. Her long golden hair fell rippling over her shoulders into his face like rays of sunlight. He held her closer still, excited but not impatient. Impatience had often been his fault in the past, but now, in the vague timelessness where they seemed suspended, there was no need. A great gust of happiness swept over him. He raised her soft face, with its wide forget-me-not eyes, and brought his lips to hers. They touched, just touched, when a piercing clarion call shook them both violently. The vision trembled before him. The violin went off key and stopped. A second trumpet blast followed. Then a third and the picture that was Helen vanished altogether. He stretched out his empty arms, but she was gone.

Kenneth woke with a lurch, still thinking of his dream.

Cheated – just when he had reached the best part. Why had he been so slow? Why must they blow that confounded horn anyway? It was too bad.

He was tired, dog tired. His masturbatory white face lay without motion or expression on the pillow. A delicious inertia encompassed him. But some strange yet familiar sense of dread was at work within him. Was something special happening today? Then with a pang he remembered. He was being sucked back with the force of gravity. Today he returned to his battalion.

In the curtained twilight of his room he saw again the hideous barracks looming out of the dark, heard the subhuman shouts and cries, felt the senseless vacancy that, enveloping everything like a yellow fog, gripped him with suspense.

How long his leave had seemed only a week ago. The last couple of days he had counted the hours. Now there were fewer than ten. He counted again. Fewer than nine!

He opened his eyes. Patches of light were flickering from the shafts of dusty sunlight shining through the slits in the curtain and making grotesque patterns on the carpet. He turned over to face the wall and curled himself into a warm protective bundle. As he was doing this he heard the voice of his father calling up to him – and realised he had not left for his office. He would soon be up there. There was nothing to be done. He would count to ten and spring from his bed. He closed his eyes, counted slowly to ten: and nothing happened. Surprised, he decided to count a further five. Again nothing. Just a minute or two more then. There could be no harm in that.

A noise, like the explosion of a far-off bomb, sounded from below. Was that his father's footsteps on the stairs? He scrambled out of bed with alarming speed, fumbled into his dressing gown inside-out and stood blinking and barefooted on the carpet. There was silence. No-one was coming up after all.

He groped around and found his slippers, emerging from his bedroom, padding across the sun-streaked landing and making his way downstairs. Warmth from the uncertain central heating below, tropical this morning, rose to console him as he descended. At the foot of the staircase he met his father on his way up to rouse him.

"Good morning, Bright Eyes," his father greeted him jovially. Then, with a bray of laughter, he began smacking his hands together like pistol shots.

Kenneth slunk by with a whisper.

Chapter 8

ONE CANNOT EAT BREAKFAST
ALL DAY

And now the family had assembled in the dining room for the ceremony of breakfast.

Henry was already pitching in; Anne was shouting incoherently to Mrs Gaff for reinforcements of food; Mrs Gaff was shouting back at Anne; Kenneth ambled in vague circles around the hall, searching for newspapers; Mathilda was frantically "finishing the sitting room" nearby; a cupboard door creaked open, closed, and Miss Tooth floated noiselessly down to her breakfast. The deep-throated sound of the news came from the trunk-like wireless, full of jaunty menace, weather, scores. And against all this, the choreography of the family was being played out as they found their places at the table. One person was missing. The ageing figure of Eustace tottered onto the landing and prepared for its journey down the Everest of stairs.

Going downwards presented something of a challenge for

Eustace. Despite numerous accidents, he refused point-blank to use the banisters, lest such an action be construed by the women in the house as a sign of senility. Instead he would sway and jerk his way down, pausing for a full ten seconds or more with his feet set wide apart on each stair, his bloodshot eyes glazed with effort and exertion, his breath coming in deep muttering gasps as he took stock of his position and prepared to lower himself further down. During his progress in either direction, all other traffic was, as a mark of respect, forbidden to pass, the delay sometimes exceeding ten minutes as the remainder of the family waited in a deferential line behind him. On this occasion it was a mere four or five minutes before he was able, with a sigh of relief, to reach the foot of the stairs and heave himself across to the dining room from where the sounds of communal feeding mixed with official pronounce-ments could be heard drifting from the half-open door. The old man stopped, swaying slightly, sullen-faced, as if trying to make out some insults from within. Then, thinking better of it, he lurched forward and peeped through a crack in the door.

At the head of the table sat Henry, inclined to fatness now, jovial and vociferous, his face veined like a sailor's, his jet-black hair like an oily sea. The dark-green suit he wore was a size too small for him and clashed deafeningly with his complexion. He bulged out of it, as he had earlier wriggled into it, the stitches taut, the buttons straining almost audibly. He ate ravenously, swallowing gigantic mouthfuls at speed.

And there, at the centre of the table, half standing, half sitting on a garden stool, was Anne. Her diminutive, almost hunchback figure was twisted towards her grandson to reveal a parchment face with its lips vividly encrimsoned in such a manner as to suggest that her mouth extended halfway across her right cheek. Her sparse metallic grey hair lay chaotic and unkempt, crushed by a dilapidated hairnet. From her left ear hung a green earring; on her right foot a sober black gumshoe. Around her neck was suspended a chain of imitation pearls that stretched, as though elastic, below her waist, and, when she got down from her stool, almost to the floor itself. For the rest, she wore an array of nondescript jerseys and pullovers, grey-orange, grey-yellow and grey-pink. Below all this paraphernalia drooped a long shapeless grey skirt which reached almost to her ankles. She had, as Mathilda often remarked, "let herself go".

Before her on the table was piled an assortment of articles, reminiscent of a junk shop. There was a ballpoint pen, a bottle of ink, some soap, a ball of string, several aspirin and a small tin of boot polish. She was prepared for all disasters.

As Eustace manoeuvred himself into the room, Kenneth shuffled towards his place at the table. With his dressing gown still inside out, his hair swept low over his eyes which were themselves half closed, his ears projecting like vegetables, Kenneth did not look his best in the morning. He did not feel his best. His long thin body was bent, his face bleached of all colour save a faint greenness. He was a great tribulation to his grandmother.

Stopping for a moment by the dining-room window, which gave on to the frosted lawn outside, he saw his great-aunt Mathilda, almost six feet tall and lightly clad as if for tennis, scattering bread and butter with bits of cherry cake for the birds that flocked eagerly around her. She did this partly for the sake of the worms. Her wizened features, mottled and spotted like some Spanish omelette, were creased with worry. For although Mathilda preferred eating with the birds and would always take her breakfast out to the garden, she could not prevent her thoughts from straying back to the family indoors. What a spectacle they made! How much fresher and cleaner it was to be outside, under the sky, the wind, the sleet, the snow, away from all that meaningless chatter. Anne was such a messy eater, she thought, as she expertly flicked the bread and cake hither and thither. Eustace too, poor man, produced a terrible clatter with those dentures of his, though he never heard it himself of course, being so deaf. As for Kenneth, he had no table manners at all. But Henry was the worst. He actually talked about food while he was eating – monologues about English cheeses, German sausages, French wines. And all this because he'd been in the navy and travelled to places.

In summer Mathilda enjoyed being in the garden out of sight of everyone and inhaling as much fresh air as possible with which to carry on the day. She simply couldn't understand *certain persons* who stuck indoors and crept around all day like mice. You wouldn't believe the difficulty she had in dragging her brother outdoors sometimes. From Anne she expected no better.

Unaware of these thoughts, everyone in the dining room had stopped eating and was regarding Eustace. The old man's benevolent features beamed suspiciously round the table, passing over them yet somehow leaving the impression that he had noticed no-one. He stood just inside the room with the door flapping behind him like the rudder of a boat, stock-still as if struggling to recollect who all these people gathered to meet him might be.

Eustace was over six feet tall, but his back was badly cracked by time and his withered arms hung lifelessly down the sides of his drooping body. His ancient grey flannels, by now formless, were hitched up tight almost to his armpits by a pair of short braces. He was unshaven and his spectacles threatened to tumble down from the difficult position they held at the extreme of his nose. On top of his almost wholly bald head a large blood clot was visible, like an extinct volcano, at the spot where he repeatedly knocked himself on the corner of the sitting-room mantelpiece when adjusting the television. The loose green knot of his tie was caught halfway up his chest. He wore in addition a new ill-fitting cardigan, a birthday present from his wife who always gave her presents well in advance of the correct date so that she could complain, when the actual day arrived, that she had nothing to give owing to the family's chronic lack of money.

Eustace and Kenneth found their ways simultaneously to their places. Circumspect and unhurried, they appeared to be moving in a well-rehearsed ballet. They glided quietly, each on his separate route, like sleepwalkers against a rhythmic babbling from Anne.

"Good morning, both of you. Your eyes, Kenneth, look like two burnt holes in a blanket. You can have a banana if you want. Your grapefruit isn't at all good, I'm afraid. I've done the best I can, but that Mrs Gaff is as much use as a sick headache. She can't cook for coffee. You'll really have to speak to her, Eustace. Kenneth, you look like a dying duck in a thunder-storm. The marmalade's at your right elbow, Eustace – I mean Henry, so don't say I didn't tell you. Tea, Eustace? There isn't a single spoon in the house . . ."

Kenneth sat down next to Miss Tooth. There she was, her dead white hair screwed tightly round to the back of her head where it was strangled and knotted into a small hard bun. She peered inquisitively through her thin silver-rimmed spectacles at haddock in a sea of watery butter before her. A tidy eater, Miss Tooth. No question of that. With what fastidious deli-cacy did she tinker with her defenceless prey before making the vital incision and conveying a morsel towards her firmly sealed mouth. Then snap! Her angular jaws pounced and seized upon the fragment.

There was something sinister about Miss Tooth. She sat well back and solidly entrenched in her chair, her spine upright, her old black shoes appearing nailed to the ground. She was dressed, as on every weekday, in a plain brown cardigan completely buttoned up under her neat pepper-and-salt suit. In some ways she resembled a piece of Victorian furniture. She gave the air of someone who had arrived on the planet in this present form and clothing. When she perambulated across the room to fetch her tea, she held herself in a curiously tilted angle, her vast hindquarters protruding to the rear while the top portion of her body inclined inflexibly forward so that it seemed she must, in spite of all past experience, fall on her face. But when she rested in her chair, she sat there as if for all eternity, so silent, so correct, with an air of reproach about her.

Eustace subsided with a deep groan onto the soft inflatable life belt without which he could not manage. "I wish you'd all go away," he gently sighed. Then he held up his finger for silence.

Chapter 9

MENUS

Every meal in This'll Do was like a game of musical chairs.

Anne, for the very life of her, could never remain in the same chair for long, but would saunter indecisively around the room clockwise or anti-clockwise as the spirit moved her, humming slightly, altering the position of the plates on the table by a fraction this way or that, and then, after a pause, back again to where they had been before she touched them. Now and then she would settle, perhaps on her own garden chair or on Eustace's life belt or even occasionally on the window sill – it was impossible to forecast which. There seemed no pattern to her actions and she irritated everyone including herself.

Eustace, too, would sometimes take it into his head to wander off during the course of a meal, to shave or pull some chain, or switch off a light he remembered (incorrectly) having left on in the garage the day before, or to wrestle in secret with his truss, his bandages, his dentures – and would not be seen again till after the meal was over. Then he would suddenly re-appear demanding whether the food would ever be ready.

Henry would rise from his chair to instruct the assembled family, put them right on one or two matters. Striding up and down the length of the dining room and turning around at each end, he would advance his opinions of celluloid, cricket, driving or naval strategy.

Kenneth would jump up suddenly and dash upstairs to fetch some book from his bedroom where, several hours later, his distraught grandmother would find him immersed in his reading or his dreams.

As for Mathilda, she was late for the few meals she did come to. She ate very little, very quickly, catching up, overtaking and finishing before everyone else. She ate with a faint look of distaste spread over her honest features – and afterwards drank large quantities of soda water which, she explained, "cleans one out inside".

Back in the good old days, even before Churchill came to power and while the family still had some money, Mathilda had kept a cellar of spa waters in the attic: bottles of Evian and Perrier, Vichy and Pellegrino. Apart from a little weak Negus and some camomile tea in the afternoon, this was all she drank. She gave the impression that she was waiting for the day when capsules, washed down with a glass of mineral water, would suffice. Until that pleasant day arrived, she submitted reluctantly to the crude assortment of things put in front of her. The only person who met with her approval was Miss Tooth. The economy and quietness of her performance at table were irreproachable. Nothing short of a landmine would disturb her.

Chapter 10

REASON NOT THE NEED

Eustace held his finger up for silence. He bent down, twisted some knobs – and another newscast sounded from the radio: an earthquake in Peru; war between reds and whites, blacks and yellows with their casualty totals; disaster in the air; fire on the ocean; threat of a General Strike; death on the Cheshire roads; the length of a skirt; Royalty opens clinic; Australia all out; cloudy with intervals.

From this miscellany, they chose weather and, over the grapefruit, over the haddock, lamented it, tore it to pieces. Eustace led this assault, but Anne, soon tiring of it, switched to Royalty.

"I hope our poor Queen's not ill again."

No answer.

"She might easily succumb to sinusitis. A slip of a girl like her must take good care and use disinfectants. I expect her ministers see to that. If anything did happen I dread where we'd be with those bally Russians."

Silence.

"She must come into contact with all sorts of germ-carriers, poor lady. I think she's jolly plucky, opening those clinics. It's a wonder she doesn't catch more."

Still nothing.

The trouble was that poor Eustace couldn't hear anything these days. He'd forgotten to shave again, Anne noticed. He'd never been the same since those blackguards had got control of the country. It made one wonder what it was all for, joining the Home Guard and investing in things. She couldn't figure out what was wrong, but she knew they weren't right.

"Have you washed properly, Kenneth?" she suddenly heard herself ask.

"No."

Sometimes she thought he never did. Was he joking, she wondered. Or had they brought him up wrong?

Kenneth stared absent-mindedly out of the window where Mathilda was having her breakfast and watching the birds have theirs. Suddenly she darted away.

Anne opened her mouth to say something – she couldn't think what – when the dining-room door was flung open and a figure rushed in brandishing the newspapers.

Mathilda skidded to a halt, dropped to her knees, and began barking. Her sharp staccato yelps, released from the front of her lips, were addressed to the prostate Smith in his bed in the corner of the room. With a dog's sigh, he looked up at her and, gathering strength to reply, gave a feeble thump of his tail. It was enough. Mathilda rose.

Then she was on the move again. With a curt "Good morning!" she strode forward, smacking the newspapers down on the table next to Eustace. Jerked awake by the detonation, the old man raised his head and gazed vacantly around him. His eyes focused on the bundle in front of him, he sought *The Times* and disappeared behind it.

Mathilda prowled the room, then vanished through the doorway to the kitchen carrying Eustace's unfinished plate of haddock in one hand and Kenneth's half-eaten grapefruit in the other. The next instant she reappeared. "Smith was very ill again last night. He needs a vet." She spoke with quick formality.

A look of absolute incredulity passed over Eustace's features. *The Times* fell from his fingers and slid from his knees to the floor. The strength of his feeling bewildered him. He did not know why he should feel so shocked. He could not remember how, when he was a boy, his dog Tim had been needlessly put to sleep by a vet. His mind had forgotten the monstrous sense of injustice; but his feelings remembered – and they now called out in anguish. He twisted awkwardly round to confront his sister. For a moment he appeared unable to form a sentence. In little more than a whisper, he asked: "Needs *what?*"

Mathilda squared herself to face him. She was trembling slightly. "A vet. Needs a vet."

"Now look here," Eustace began patiently, "just you listen to me for a second and I'll tell you what's wrong with the old boy." He turned, whistled encouragingly through his teeth at the dog, and turned again. "You see . . ."

But she dared not let him finish. In a desperate and weary voice she continued, "He was sick again last night. It cannot go on like this. I'm at my wits' end. Something must be done."

"That dog gives Mathilda a frightful load of work," broke in Anne. "It can't be doing her any earthly good, being up night after night like this. She needs a holiday. We all need a holiday."

"*Really!*" protested Mathilda.

"May I get a word in for a change?" Eustace inquired.

"Oh yes, of course," snapped Mathilda. "I *was* forgetting my place. Sorry I spoke. He's only my dog, Smith."

"In spite of everything I have been trying to tell you," Eustace stubbornly resumed, "in spite of everything, it's evident you still don't understand. You know my opinion of vets – or you should by now . . ."

"Yes, Eustace," Mathilda sighed, clenching her fist. "I am perfectly well aware of your opinions, thank you."

"If that's going to be your attitude, then . . ."

"There's no call for you to shout. We *are* in the same room, you know." As she spoke, Mathilda lowered her voice to a whisper. It was a devastating change of tactics.

He leant forward but could not hear her. Through long practice Mathilda had come to judge with great accuracy what volume she should use on such occasions.

"I don't agree," Eustace replied. It seemed a fairly safe statement.

"Sorry, sorry, sorry, sorry," chanted Mathilda, staring most unsorrowfully up at the ceiling.

Anne had slipped from her chair and was limping over to Smith's bed. "Poor thing. Keeping Mathilda up all hours of the night."

"Really, Anne," exclaimed Mathilda automatically. But the fire had gone out of her voice and she looked old with worry. What was to be done? She could not let the matter rest there. She resolved that something really must be done that very day.

Chapter 11

REHEARSAL AND DISPERSAL

It was Mathilda who began it. "I'm off to do the plates now," she announced.

She ran for the doorway, but a scream from Anne stopped her. "Now do be sensible. Do leave those things, Mathilda," she begged. "You're in no fit state. I'll see to everything later – and so will Mrs Gaff."

Then the quarrelling began.

"Do it later? Is that what you said? How much later? A week? Two months? I'd like to see it – I really should."

There was a rustle of paper as Eustace disappeared behind *The Times*. The rest of the family listened in a dazed silence like people who had heard it so many times before that they had grown stupefied. They sat in profound yet tranquil dismay, bowed, overcome. There was a weariness too about both protagonists that suggested they were in rehearsal for the real performance, under contract to mouth these lines, and that these roles filled them with overwhelming distaste. They seemed powerless as actors on stage to alter what was taking place. The words flowed from them mechanically as if they were under a spell.

"I insist that you leave those blessed things alone," Anne persisted.

Mathilda inhaled deeply and rubbed a hand across her eyes. "I'd save yourself the trouble if I were you." The formula sounded from her lips without any choice or effort of will. "In any case I'd have to do them all again afterwards, as you well know."

This was a favourite card of Mathilda's and she produced it with the full knowledge that she had played an ace, a momentary shadow of pleasure flickering across her face.

"Oh you're so *obstinate*, Mathilda." Anne shook her head dizzily.

"Obstinate, am I?" queried Mathilda as if this was the first time she had heard such an extraordinary charge. "That's rich, coming from you of all people, I must say. Obstinate!"

"Bitch!"

"Ha! Ha! How perfectly charming. You improve on yourself every day."

The time was now ready for widening the debate. Miss Tooth cleared her throat for combat.

"No thank you, Miss Tooth," called out Mathilda who had been waiting for this. "I know what you're going to say, but I couldn't hear of it in any circumstances. There is no need for you to put yourself out."

"Put herself out?" Anne repeated with a derisive laugh. "When has she ever put herself out?"

"Really!" protested Mathilda, high pitched in scorn. "How dare you speak like that! Sometimes I believe you should be certified."

"Perhaps I should," Anne agreed inconsequentially.

A lull fell over the breakfasters, a deep and exhausted pause. They looked round the table from one to the other with dazed expressions, each one furtively hoping that a truce had been called. But they knew it could not be. The matter had to be thrashed out. Miss Tooth again cleared her throat.

"Oh for Christ's sake, don't you do it as well, Toothy," exploded Henry.

Eustace did not enter the argument by word of mouth, but *The Times* trembled with more agitation when some candidates took the floor than others, and from this a skilled observer might register the intensity of his feelings.

Then Kenneth piped up facetiously: "I know. Let's all of us wash the plates!"

There was a rustle of paper as Eustace raised the shaking newspaper in the air, allowing one corner of it to rest in his tea and draw up the brown fluid into a soggy arc round the print. Kenneth had offered an unrehearsed interruption, and Mathilda looked quite upset. But Henry roared with laughter, rocking backwards and forwards so that the others began to fear for his chair. "Splendid idea, old boy! Splendid!"

Most surprising of all was Miss Tooth's behaviour. Producing a spotless white handkerchief from her sleeve, she put it up to her spectacles and began swaying to and fro in feeble imitation of Henry.

"God's truth!" Henry burst out, looking at his watch. He would have gone on, but before he could draw breath Mathilda went into action, clutching wildly at her throat. "It's like an oven in here," she gasped. "For heaven's sake let's have some air before it's too late." No-one moved – then she swept across the room and started banging open the windows.

This was a sign for the rest of the family to disperse.

"Well, I must be off," murmured Eustace as if contemplating a long journey.

"And so must I," agreed Henry urgently. "It's an important day for me."

The family rose from their chairs and hurried out of the icy room.

Chapter 12

REFLECTIONS OF A MOTORIST

Before "quitting the precincts" as he put it, Henry cornered his son who would have left for the army by the time his father returned from the office. "Cheerio, old boy," he said, clapping him on the arm. "I don't suppose it's too bad now. Six months to do, is it?"

"Ten months still, I'm afraid."

Henry chuckled. "Oh well, that's no lifetime. Anyway," he went on, injecting a sterner note into his voice, "remember what I said to you last night. I want a sensible decision out of you pretty soon about your future. A choice of career cannot be taken too early these days, mark my words."

Kenneth gave a hopeless nod.

Henry hesitated in the doorway, anxious to be off but wanting to say something reassuring to his son. "Are you alright for money still?" he asked gruffly.

Kenneth said that he was alright.

"Now don't be an utter fool, Kenneth. Don't be a simpleton.

You don't want to leave yourself short, do you?" Even at his kindest, Henry managed to sound offensive. He was shy of his own generosity, awkward at exposing his good nature. "Here you are. You'd better take this three quid. That should keep you off the rocks for the time being – and talking of rocks, *tempus fugit*. I must be wending my merry way."

"Thanks."

"Now I really must be off," repeated Henry who always, it seemed, said goodbye before introducing some new line of conversation. He shuffled further out and blew into his hands. "When will you be able to get some more leave and grace us with your presence again, do you suppose?"

"Next leave I will have to be in Lancashire."

"I see," Henry said shortly. It was natural enough, he thought, that the boy should want to see his mother. Even if she had been the guilty party, even if she had seen more of him in the early days, even if it seemed unfair, Henry never made a point of complaining. He edged out on to the path. "Remember to keep in touch with us occasionally – tell us all the scrapes you get into."

"He never tells us a mortal thing," complained Anne, who had been listening to them out of sight and who now came wandering out with a duster in her hand. "If he was sent abroad to fight in some rotten war, I don't think we'd ever find out."

Henry, with his hand on the gate, felt obliged to comment. He pondered gravely. "I must confess he never waxes what one might call eloquent concerning his own actions in life." He opened the gate, balanced himself momentarily on the curb, and with a sudden boisterous wave let out a "cheerio!" and was gone.

It was always a bit of relief to be at the wheel and ponder over things in comparative peace for a spell. For the first twelve and a half miles of his twenty-five mile drive to the office, he tended to deliberate over family affairs; while for the last half of his journey the question of celluloid occupied his mind. It was vice versa on his return journey.

His mind that morning was particularly crowded with thoughts – not all of them pretty ones. The whole family, he reflected grimly, would soon drive him cuckoo.

Take the old man for example. Years ago he'd been quite a lad – and a bloody fine athlete into the bargain. Had it not been for his father, the brigadier general, he might have turned out a damn good oar. But the general had been a bit too keen on him pursuing his studies, forgetting, it seemed, that a spot of sport can assist a man no end in the world of commerce. A Blue, even these days, meant something.

How the old man had eventually found his way into corned beef remained one of those baffling mysteries that defeat all reason and research. He'd gone out to Canada, met mother, and immediately married her. In due course, back in Cheshire, his parents had died – first his mother a few years after the birth of Mathilda, and then the general shortly after Henry's own birth. Suddenly the full burden of family responsibility descended on Eustace.

Two miles.

Not only had the old man lost most of his money, but recently he was losing hold of his faculties. All evening he sat in front of that new television regardless of what was on. And he such a fine oar once! What was one to make of it?

He was becoming extraordinarily forgetful. Every time he mislaid his spectacles, he would blame everyone within earshot of criminal theft. And all the time, flitting around him like flies, were the women: mother wailed as if she were being tortured and Mathilda chanted her obviously insincere apologies. What a bloody pantomime they put on!

Four miles.

Mathilda he used to admire before he'd returned to live at This'll Do. Trouble was, of course, that unlike him she'd never married. Naturally no man worth his salt enjoys being looked down on, and her unusual height had been a distinct disadvantage from the start, poor girl. Yet so charming was her personality, so delightful her smile that she had scores of eligible men buzzing round her. A number of them became Henry's friends. There was a joke (a joke in rather poor taste) that one of them might end up as his "uncle". But Mathilda, though always friendly, never seemed to fancy any of them in particular – until that little Italian came on the scene. Overnight, as it were, she became engaged to him. Everyone was thunderstruck – even Henry himself had been rocked on his heels. Mathilda, he was sure, could have done better for herself. The fellow looked such a little popinjay when seen against her. It was a ridiculous arrangement. To cap it all, he spoke hardly a single intelligible word of English. How they communicated was a mystery. Then the war had come, Emilio disappeared to Italy and wrote to Mathilda calling it all off. You could see his point. But she had never come across him again since the war. A poor effort, Henry thought, unless of course the poor chap had been killed.

Mathilda had taken the whole wretched little affair most sensibly at the time, though any fool could see the very bottom had been knocked out of her world, poor kid. But she refused to let it get her down for long – unlike most females.

Later on Henry noticed how Mathilda had picked up the habit of feeding the birds which gathered as regularly as clockwork to have their meals on the lawn. And if they were kept hanging about, what a shindy they would set up! It had been Mrs Gaff, to do her justice, who had drawn his attention to their ferocious chorus. He could remember Mathilda standing at the window and watching them as they swooped from the shivering branches, darted low over the garden, landed and began hopping about the grass. Three meals a day those birds had served to them, and cake for tea.

To cut a long story short it hadn't taken Henry two shakes of a monkey's tail to put two and two together. The birds, he reckoned, had taken the Italian's place in Mathilda's affections. He didn't mind admitting that he thought it a change for the better. Nor did it take him a lifetime to tumble to the fact that Mathilda was bent on spending the remainder of her time taking care of the old people. One couldn't help admiring her.

After due deliberation, during which he rejected the notion of a parrot, Henry hit on the bright idea of presenting her with Smith – a plain, honest-to-god English dog. Since that time, Mathilda's life had revolved round the animal, morning, noon and night. She was late for meals on account of Smith's walks; she was rude to countless individuals in defending the dog where no-one had intended criticism; she put off practically all engagements until there were none left. But all the while she grew more irritable and bitter. She was growing old, it seemed, before her time.

Seven miles.

As for Anne, she had come bitterly to resent Miss Tooth's position in the house. Some might feel sorry for his mother, but when one was forced to listen to her, day in day out, carrying on the same moaning monologue, it became a different kettle of fish. Of course she was bored to bloody tears, they all knew that. Henry *was* sorry for her in a way – or would have been had she not been so damned sorry for herself.

Fact was that, like so many silly little girls, she'd expected a miracle to take place the second her marriage ceremony was over – and the rest of her life had been a disappointment. She was, however, genuinely fond of the boy. Kenneth really could do no wrong in her eyes. If Henry himself put a foot out of line just once, he heard about it till kingdom come. But Kenneth could get away with sheer bloody murder.

Yet the real trouble was Kenneth himself. It was frightening to contemplate what an awful cropper he might come if he didn't watch his step. A bright future stretched before him in corned beef, and if Henry's thirty-odd years of experience counted for anything, he'd be on the Board before he'd reached the wrong side of fifty. But the fact that the job would involve the boy spending twenty years or more out in Canada, a country he might otherwise never have the good fortune to see, actually seemed to discourage him. He preferred to kick his heels in the north of England. If the old man found out how Kenneth felt, it would break his heart.

Naturally there was always celluloid. But even here Kenneth was unenthusiastic. Whenever Henry did manage to pin him down, he behaved like a cornered animal. But then no-one could really pin him down. He lived in some airy-fairy dreamland of his own invention, altogether unrelated to modern commercial reality. His head was full of music and literature – all very well so far as they went, but neither of them could provide one's daily bread. Kenneth would kick himself later if he mucked up everything. God's truth, the heavy Victorian father was a trifle out of Henry's line, but he couldn't neglect his responsibilities altogether.

Nine miles.

Matters had come to a head between them the previous night. Henry felt obliged to point out that there was no sense in affecting to despise hard cash. Better to be miserable in comfort than in hardship. Kenneth could not expect to spend his life running round concert halls and libraries. They led nowhere. If he wanted to write, he would do so whatever job he took. Certainly it was good to have a hobby, but Henry very much doubted whether he would apply himself to serious scribbling and produce a few tomes. Yet he was luckier than most. If he played his cards right, he'd be sitting pretty by the time he was Henry's age.

Henry didn't want to be a killjoy – even his worst enemy wouldn't accuse him of that. He wasn't so decrepit that he couldn't remember what it felt like to be young. Indeed, at heart, he still *was* young, damned young for a man of his age. But these days, young people had to put in a bit of fact-facing, a little getting-down-to-brass-tacks, if you please. The arts were fine enough, but no-one would care for them much in the future. At the present moment of going to press everyone craved sex and excitement – same as the Roman Empire before *that* fell to pieces. The future lay with the scientists – if there was to be a future. And if Kenneth didn't want to get trampled underfoot, he'd simply have to knuckle down and climb abroad the bandwagon as best he could.

Twelve miles.

Henry had spelt all this out last night. But what was the use? His son merely studied the carpet under his feet, occasionally smiling as if to signal that he, Henry, had announced something particularly inane, even for a parent. So, in desperation, he had talked on and on into the night, about sentiment in the corned beef market, about mergers in celluloid, and then about one thing and about another thing, and then one thing again and again, until both their heads were lolling with weariness and they climbed exhausted to their beds.

Of course Henry didn't want to bully the boy. But Kenneth was so short-sighted – rather like Old Harris and young Belcher at the office. Born in blinkers, they must have been. Take that merger, for instance . . .

Twelve and a half miles.

Chapter 13

CRISIS

While Henry was pondering his way to the office, much feverish activity had been taking place at This'll Do.

Shooed out of the dining room, the kitchen, the sitting room and the lavatory by Mathilda's flailing dusters, Anne had come temporarily to rest in the garage. In every room they had become involved in lightning quarrels. Never had Anne seen Mathilda so fierce.

Fantasies of how she might introduce a vet into the house without the knowledge of Eustace mantled Mathilda's brain. She would smuggle one in while her brother was down in the village; she would introduce one to him as the brother of a school friend she had not set eyes on for years; she would pretend to sprain her ankle while out walking and explain that the kind gentleman had helped her back home; she would pretend he was the new Conservative candidate; she would lead him through the back way so that no-one would ever know. But then common sense reasserted itself and each scheme seemed more impractical than the last. What was she to do?

It was to work off this frustration and a feeling of disloyalty to Eustace that she was acting so aggressively this morning. Even Miss Tooth shied away from her and went to sit by Smith in the dining room.

Having driven Anne out of the house, Mathilda bounded upstairs. Anne, loitering amid the bicycles, heard her stamping feet ascending and heaved a sigh. Picking up her cargo of odds and ends in an overflowing bag of old biscuits, hairpins, hatpins and the stubs of cheque books, she ambled back into the house and began banging the cushions into new shapes. Mathilda, upstairs in the bathroom, overheard her. She turned off the taps, pulled her clothes back on, and raced downstairs. Anne braced herself for the encounter and they met at the foot of the stairs. For a brief second the two women eyed each other keenly, as skilled opponents in a highly complex game. Something almost like respect for the other's powers seemed to mingle with their obvious enmity. Then the battle for the hall opened. Mathilda was winning; Mathilda would have won, but before she could rout her enemy, a weird and unearthly scream brought them both to a stop.

Only eight hours now, but Kenneth had not resigned himself. He had hoped for a railway strike, for an Act of God, for a deplorable accident or disease. If he ate soap or feigned illness, he would still need a doctor's certificate – and he could hardly manage that any more easily than Mathilda could get hold of a vet.

He climbed the stairs to his bedroom and lay down. Mathilda thought he didn't care for the dog. But that wasn't really true. What was true was that he hated talking about suffering and illness. Placed as Smith was in the dining room, the whole family was obliged to sit around and contemplate him slowly expiring. And how they talked about his symptoms of debility and sickness! As if to confirm the worst of what was being spoken, the old dog panted and coughed and flicked his tail to hear his name being so often mentioned. Even when he was fit he monopolised the conversation at practically every meal: where he had been on his walks, the actual paths, the fields, the particular trees, the exact nature of and the precise spot where he had "done his business", its colour, consistency and volume: all was eagerly discussed.

Smith trusted the family: but they were powerless to help him now. Kenneth felt his predicament keenly. He belonged to two worlds, being schooled in the routines and activities of human beings yet with the instincts still of an animal and wholly at home in neither world. Smith loved his comfort – warmth, plenty of good food, a soft bed, endless attention – just as any human being might. He had come to expect it, to need it. Yet sometimes as he lay stretched out on the divan, encircled by all sorts of appetising titbits, the object of everyone's lavish affections, and for all the world content with his lot, the bark of a faraway dog, bounding free across the common, would sound faintly through the air and penetrate the sanctum of This'll Do. And then Smith would prick up his ears and a wistful look would show in his eyes as he stood in the dining room, trembling and erect, his tail extended, his head on one side straining to catch more intoxicating sounds. Sometimes he whined a little or gave a few of his indoor barks, which would send Anne bustling off to open the front door to no-one, saying all the time what a fine house dog he was. But it seemed to Kenneth that to give him extra cake and pat him and call him "a good boy" was to lend oneself to a conspiracy of misunderstanding.

He looked again at his watch. Just seven hours left now. He got up intending to put on a record. But before he could reach the record player, a piercing cry came from below, and he stood muted to the spot, his heard thumping.

Eustace had also heard the shout and recognised it as coming from Miss Tooth. He lunged out of the sitting room but on reaching the doorway of the dining room, became incoherently involved in a silent, heated scrimmage carried on with Anne. Kenneth, hurrying cautiously down the stairs, was just in time to see Eustace employing his extra height to advantage, to get through the door.

Mathilda was already there, kneeling on the floor. Smith, who had collapsed while trying to walk a few paces, lay flat on the floor like a black pool in front of her. After the first stab of anguish, the shock was making her loquacious. Something, she kept on repeating, would have to be done. Eustace or no Eustace, Smith would see a vet. She began crying.

While Eustace was endeavouring to come to grips with the situation, Miss Tooth tiptoed out to make her a little soothing Bovril. Anne, pottering around the perimeter of the room suddenly noticed Kenneth pop his head quickly round the door and then, even more quickly, withdraw it again. He was a funny child, Kenneth. Not fond of dogs in the least – which was not, in her opinion, a very healthy sign. He'd actually said one day that he preferred cats! But then, if she remembered rightly, there was that mother of his. Helga – such a silly name, Anne thought – was some sort of foreigner, and this probably accounted for a lot. Foreign blood could do funny things. She was said to have come from quite a good family in her own country, wherever that was. But it's never quite the same thing. She had created a lot of mischief – and suddenly Anne shouted out, telling Kenneth just that.

Eustace stood there looking from Smith to Mathilda and shaking his head. It was a puzzle certainly. But better not to make a fuss. Mathilda's voice cut through his thoughts. "Smith has had a setback," he heard her say. "I think it would be wise for us to call in a second opinion."

This phrase appealed to Eustace. He turned it over in his mind. Who could they ask? There was old Colonel Humblemere, of course, Mathilda might like that. After all he had a dog of his own and might know something. His sister was obviously "not herself" and it was probably best to go along with her. "Very well then," he replied. "Call in whoever you like." The words, which had been so difficult for him to say, gave him an involuntary sense of relief. He repeated them.

Mathilda looked incredulous. "Do you mean," she began, sounding almost indignant, "that you'd arrange for someone to come here?"

"Certainly I would," Eustace answered easily.

"A vet – for Smith?"

Eustace suddenly felt angry. So they'd tricked him. He could see their game now. The whole thing had been staged. If he said no, they'd maintain he hadn't heard or hadn't understood. They'd say he was getting senile. But he wasn't having any of that. He wandered towards the door, turned and shouted: "Yes, I've said so, haven't I?"

For the next half hour, kneeling beside Smith, Mathilda waited while her brother blundered about the house. He was like an angry elephant. He made no telephone call and he didn't go out. But he was an honourable man. Mathilda knew he would not go back on his word. She would have to remind him a little later once he'd cooled down. That was all.

Smith in fact seemed rather better. Mathilda retired to the

kitchen to sip her Bovril and be comforted by the silence of Miss Tooth and the breezy cheerfulness of Mrs Gaff. All the aggression had fled out of her. She felt tired.

Chapter 14

A SMALL TALE

As he dressed, Kenneth found himself thinking over his grandmother's words about Helga.

These days she had practically no contact with This'll Do beyond a formal exchange of Christmas cards each year.

In the past she had presented a striking contrast to the Farquhar family. She had the habit of saying something to a person's face and then something entirely contradictory behind his back, both statements being untrue and neither availing her in any way. She was spoken of as being jolly good company by north-country businessmen who generally bored her. At parties she often found it difficult knowing what to say to people, but somehow the words flowed and if the drink was flowing too, her eyes would become mysteriously indecipherable, her actions more erratic than erotic (perhaps a bit of both). The next morning it all seemed so unreal, so unlike herself, that she could scarcely believe there had been a party.

At This'll Do she still had the reputation of being a bad

lot, someone who was up to no good, and she was usually referred to anonymously as "that woman". But to others, in rather different circumstances, she appeared a sophisticated woman of the world and a good sport. It was strange that someone so fundamentally simple could assume so many reputations. To Kenneth, her only son, she was a problem.

Since her divorce from Henry, Helga had remarried approximately three times. Her first husband, a fellow Swiss, whom she described as manly, had eventually died in bed. Her third, a Scottish businessman named Rory whom she described as sensible, separated from her soon after their honeymoon. He had wanted a later marriage to gain maximum tax advantage and five days golfing at Gleneagles. But she had swept this plan aside, advancing the date of their marriage and spending their honeymoon on an island in the South Atlantic which had been recommended to her by a very helpful military gentleman whom she met when bicycling in the country. Still innocently charmed at this early stage of their relationship by Helga's whims, Rory had agreed to this. In any event, he reasoned, Helga had more experience of honeymoons than he did.

They were surprised on disembarking to be greeted by the stranger who had assisted Helga with her tyres when she was out bicycling – especially Rory, who had never heard of him and was confused by his wife's whispered explanations. The stranger introduced himself as Colonel Salamander, deputy commander of the military forces stationed on the island. He insisted on accompanying them to their villa. Next morning Rory rose early and decided to explore the island while Helga, as was her custom, had a light breakfast in bed.

She had barely finished her orange juice when she heard rifle shots accompanied by some smothered Scottish cries. She thought no more of it until, later that morning, Colonel Salamander knocked politely at the door and informed her that her husband had been discovered in a military installation surrounded on all sides by large signs written in the local patois warning people to stay out. He had been placed under arrest and confined to quarters close to the villa. The Colonel had come to fetch some of his clothing and shaving equipment. Helga herself was free to go where she liked providing she was escorted by the Colonel.

Helga was stunned. It was too inconsiderate of Rory. She felt ashamed of him. The Colonel assured her that he was doing everything he could to get her husband released. Unfortunately his superior was a difficult man – and he spoke no English.

The next two weeks were the worst in Rory's life. He was comfortably housed, well fed, but always under guard. Although not permitted to see or speak to his wife, he could in fact see her sometimes through his window and hear her at the villa usually in the company of the Colonel. He heard them laughing, saw her once or twice waving and smiling. Alone in his single-pillowed bedroom he lay awake listening to them – the clink of glasses, the sounds of merriment, floating in on the soft night air. If he hadn't known better, he would have thought they were enjoying themselves. What was going on? The silences were worst of all.

After a dozen days and nights, Colonel Salamander visited Rory and told him that his superior had yielded to his appeal for clemency and that he and Helga were free to go – providing they did so on the boat which was departing that very morning. Rory staggered out into the sunlight like a drunken man. Helga appeared preoccupied. The Colonel escorted them on to the boat and waved them off to the music of a military brass band.

On their way home Rory made some attempt to gather his scattered faculties and demand an explanation from his wife. But she was in no mood for cross-examination. A fine husband he had been, deserting her on their honeymoon. She had to be civil to that military reptile for Rory's sake – and his veiled insinuations were all the thanks she got. She burst into tears.

It was on the boat that his symptoms began. He would cry repeatedly in his sleep to be "let out". Helga was hardly able to get a wink of sleep. Back home he became worse, banging on open doors while making the same demand. She took him to Gleneagles but he demanded to be "let out" even on the golf course. Eventually he was put in a Home where he joined other inmates begging to be let out. On the grounds of separation Helga eventually divorced him – and at last he was let out.

Helga's present husband Mr Finsbury Roach, whom she

described as sweet, was something in industrial fertiliser. On their marriage he had sought occasion to dictate a letter to his secretary urging Kenneth never to cease venerating Helga, his new wife, as the woman who had given him birth, albeit through the agency of someone other than himself.

By this time Helga had become disconcertingly vague, often calling her new husband by the first name of one of her previous husbands. Mr Roach would shake his head several times with surprising violence, like a cat with something in its ear. And all at once he looked old.

Helga's dog, a small black Scotty that answered sometimes to the name Tonk, had adjusted himself better and also responded to the word Smith.

This misuse of names Helga extended to her friends and those of her husband. By mischance many of them had surnames that might have served as first names. There were Mr and Mrs Charles, Mr and Mrs Thomas, the Walters, the Williamses, Captain and Mrs Norman, Commander James and several others. Helga's well-intended greetings on the telephone – "Hello James", "Good morning, Thomas" and so on – had an abruptness that was greeted with silence, making her vigorously shake the phone in frustration as if this was its fault.

She had married Finsbury Roach on the advice of her young hairdresser who was herself marrying for the security it would bring her. What, Helga reasoned, could be more secure than manure – the words actually rhymed. It was a good omen, an encouraging echo – though Finsbury himself never used such a vulgar word. But not long after their marriage she found security intolerably boring.

To take her mind off it, she undertook a number of jobs – model and black-market smuggler being two of them. She embarked on smuggling in collaboration with her cook, a fiery Spaniard. He collected the "goods" and she sorted them out in the airing cupboard while Mr Roach was at the office deep in artificial fertiliser. At first the goods were mainly crockery and gin, but then the Spaniard brought in a quantity of drugs and syringes – and Helga put her foot down. The Spaniard was banished to the kitchen and the booty remained in the airing cupboard.

Most days she went out shopping. She would buy anything that caught her attention, anything she liked the look of. These shopping adventures were fun. Sometimes she got lost a few hundred yards from her home and had to take a taxi back; often she would have lunch with strangers she bumped into in the shops – and never saw again. Her eyes would sparkle with amusement at the diversity of life going on all around her. But when she came back to her luxurious mansion which she had decorated herself at great expense, she was overcome with boredom again.

Mr and Mrs Roach had been married for less than a year, but their days were filled with petty bickering which he refused to acknowledge. He was like a man warming his hands before a volcano. Every marriage, he confided to his secretary, had its ups and downs and it was better to get the downs behind one early on. Their altercations, he believed, cleared the air. Not to have had them would have indicated that something was seriously wrong.

As for Helga herself, she could never tell what she was going to get up to next. Whatever she did came as a surprise to her.

Altogether, mused Kenneth, as he wandered downstairs, his mother was a problem.

Chapter 15

THE MEDIUM AND THE MESSAGE

From the cemetery at the end of the garden there floated up to This'll Do a peaceful sense of insecurity. In the drawing room Kenneth counted the twelve notes striking like dagger thrusts from the church clock. Less than six hours now. He put down *Unarmed Combat* and, noticing a letter he had written some days earlier to his mother, he picked it up from the table and put it in his pocket. Here at last was something to do, some action to lessen the suspense.

He rose from his chair, paused to listen at the door for a moment and, hearing nothing, hurried across the hall and let himself out of the front door. A feeling of relief travelled through him as he shut the gate and began walking down the street.

He had escaped unnoticed.

Seriously concerned at the number of gashes dotted over Eustace's face, the myriad cuts criss-crossing his nose and cheeks like alleged Martian canals, and the numerous tufts of blood-soaked cotton wool advancing across his chin, Henry had bought his father an electric razor the previous year for his birthday. After some experimentation, Eustace discovered that the lavatory provided the best quarters for operating this instrument. It was better even than the garage. Nevertheless it was proving quite a business manipulating this contraption satisfactorily, though he had now got the hang of it, he rather fancied. The written instructions were oddly misinformed and had at first led him astray. He thought occasionally, while in the lavatory, of writing to the manufacturers. They might be interested to hear that he had developed a special technique of his own. It was ridiculous, however, to claim that no-one could cut himself with such a gadget, however adroitly it was handled. His own, which after a year was reasonably blunt so that it took him three-quarters of an hour to complete his shaving, punctured him now and then so that his face resembled a battlefield with lean scars from his old razor interspersed with pimply blotches made by the new one. He sometimes deliberated going back to the old and tried method, but his attempts to do so had not been happy.

He barely had time to unpack the kit, draw out the intestines and fit them into the light socket dangling from the ceiling when he heard Anne's voice calling his name. He stood there motionless. Confound the woman! He was not an unreasonable man, but all this banging at doors and blowing of horns as if they inhabited a railway station was the limit. He would not be bullied and badgered like this in his own lavatory.

He began shaving. The whirr of the machine soothed his frayed nerves. He was about to manoeuvre himself towards the opposite wall so as to shave the other side of his face, when there sounded an unrestrained banging on the lavatory door followed by a loud rattling of the handle. He stayed where he was, balanced on the lavatory seat, while Anne put her ear against the door to find out what was happening. "Henry!" she cried. "I mean Eustace! Are you alright in there?"

By way of reply Eustace switched on his razor, the buzzing of which might, he prayed, drown his wife's shouts. Undeterred she cupped her hand to her mouth and went on.

"Kenneth's gone out! Do you think he'll be alright? I saw him from my window. Just wandered off without a word. Where d'you think he could be going at this time of day? Can you hear me, Eustace?"

Eustace, recognising this allusion to his deafness, was unable to maintain his silence. Above the buzzing of his razor which, in his trembling rage he had forgotten how to switch off, he roared: "Of course I can hear you. The whole street can hear you, I shouldn't wonder."

"What ought we to do, d'you think?"

"Go away!"

"So it's swearing now, is it?" Anne shouted back. She

retreated and muttered her way down the stairs to tell Mrs Gaff.

Left in peace, Eustace spent the next few minutes wrestling with the cord, rescuing the plug from the bowels of the water tank, packing up his razor and carrying out repairs to his face. But his mind was not on these operations. He was thinking how intolerable Anne was becoming. If matters didn't get better soon he would have to *speak to her*. Still, she'd had a piece of his mind this time and no mistake. Chuckling to himself, he pulled, out of habit, the plug, unlocked the door and prepared to tackle the stairs.

Ten minutes later, still chuckling, he climbed into his overcoat and made off in the direction of the village.

Usually Mathilda would have been striding over the common by this time of day with Smith at her heels. He loved the open fields, the wind in the grass. He never missed this outing, never did less than five miles. This morning she had not wanted to go out alone. But Miss Tooth insisted that a breath of fresh air would do her all the good in the world. In the meantime she promised to keep an eye on Smith herself. And, as usual, Miss Tooth had been right. Moping around the house was doing neither herself nor anyone else any good.

Across the fields where the wind was tearing at the uncut grasses and the solitary few trees creaking as they bent before it and then sprang back, the figure of Mathilda could be seen moving at a steady canter. Already she was feeling more herself. It was like a tonic, this walk. If only Eustace and Anne got out more, she felt sure they'd benefit. Anne seldom set a foot beyond the front door, and Eustace merely went down to the village, which did him no good. He was beginning to stoop dreadfully.

It was as Mathilda reached this stage in her thoughts that she came upon the familiar corseted figure of Colonel Humblemere and his dog.

Kenneth shivered at first. But he walked fast as if he were being chased. On reaching the post office, he took the letter out of his pocket and looked at it. His mother had expected to hear from him while he was on leave. He had half promised to see her. Now it was too late. She might be wondering what had happened to him. Perhaps, before posting the letter, he had better try to phone her.

Replacing the letter in his pocket, he made his way to one of the telephone booths and dialled his mother's number. He let it ring twelve times and was on the point of putting down the receiver when a man's voice answered "Ullo."

"Hello," answered Kenneth – and pressed button A.

"Ullo," the voice said again.

"Hello. This is Kenneth. Ken-neth Far-quhar." Then an idea came to him. This was probably his mother's new Italian cook

81

– the one that hadn't done the smuggling. "Is that Romeo?" he asked.

"Yes, signor. Romeo."

"Is my mother in?"

"Signor?"

"Is my . . ." for a second Kenneth seemed to forget his mother's name, ". . . is Mrs Roach in, Romeo?"

"No. The signora out shopping with hairdresser."

"Oh, I see."

"'Ave your message?"

"It's alright, Romeo. I'll just post my letter to her."

"Signor?"

"It's not important."

"Not . . .?"

". . . Important."

"What . . .?

"IMPORTANT!"

"Important."

"Yes."

As he came up the gentle hill from the village, Kenneth passed his grandfather going down. His eyes were staring cautiously at the uneven pavement, his lifeless arms attached to two empty, swaying shopping bags. Kenneth wondered whether he should accost him and offer some kind of help, but they had passed each other before he could come to a decision. His grandfather was growing very absent-minded, Kenneth reflected. He was still thinking about this when he reached the house and found he had forgotten to post his mother's letter.

Mathilda took her hat off to people who, in spite of everything, kept themselves fighting fit.

Although the family seldom spoke to Colonel Humblemere, they had been on nodding terms with him from time out of mind. Even when quite young Mathilda and Eustace had nodded to him when he came within a certain distance of them, and he would never fail to return the compliment, drawing himself up smartly and saluting. This exchange usually took place on the rough and desolate terrain of the thicket. It was an understanding they had.

The Colonel always had his spaniel, name of Cooper, at his side. They made a fine pair, Mathilda thought, both impeccably groomed. And to think he was very nearly her brother's age. Yet he held himself straight as a poker. He had never lost that military bearing – then wryly she remembered Kenneth. She stood there acknowledging his salute when something astonishing happened. The Colonel spoke.

"I see, harrumph, you've not got your dog with you today, madam. Nothing wrong, ha-hum, I trust."

It took Mathilda several seconds to recover. Then she cupped her hands and shouted back: "I'm afraid he's rather ill."

The wind howled between them. Mathilda raised her hand

to her ear, and Colonel Humblemere, misinterpreting this action, saluted again. "Damn shame," he bellowed. "I am, hmm, most sorry to hear that. Is it serious?"

He appeared so genuinely concerned that Mathilda warmed to him. She took a couple of paces forward, but resisted the temptation to advance nearer. "The vet's coming later today," she called out – and went on to give him the history of Smith's illness.

"He's a fine dog," was the Colonel's verdict, "and it's a rum business. Expect your family is, harrumph, damn cut up."

"Oh yes. Very."

A lull descended across the thicket, Cooper, his ears pricked, listening wisely at his master's heels. Mathilda glanced down at her watch and wrinkled her forehead. "I'm afraid I must be off," she apologised. "My great-nephew is catching the six o'clock train back to the army this afternoon. He is doing his National Service, you know."

"What regiment?" demanded the Colonel.

"The Red Jackets," she answered, surprised that she knew the answer.

The Colonel unsuccessfully smothered a cry of astonishment. That, he shouted excitedly across to her, was *his* old regiment. He knew the C.O. – knew his father too, come to that. Extraordinary coincidence. How was, ha-hum, her nephew enjoying himself?

Displeased by the turn the conversation had taken, Mathilda

saw no reason to lie. "I don't think he's looking forward to going back just now."

For a moment Colonel Humblemere looked puzzled. Then his face cleared. He understood. Obviously the lad didn't feel quite right deserting his aunt when the dog was so poorly. The feeling did him credit. Dev'lish awkward position. "Can I do anything?" he offered.

Mathilda, thinking he was referring now to Smith's illness, felt gratified. Perhaps he knew a good vet. "We don't really know what to do. The trouble is we don't know anyone."

The Colonel responded nobly. "I could, ha-hum, give Armstrong a call. Ask him to grant a spot of compassionate leave. That sort of thing. Exceptional circumstances and so on. Has a dog of his own, if I remember rightly. His father certainly did."

The conversation had passed out of Mathilda's control and she felt irritated by the turn it had taken – focusing on the one person in the family who had little interest in Smith. "That's very kind, but I don't think it will be necessary."

The Colonel interpreted this as referring to his strategy. But the problem fired his imagination, involving as it did his two interests in life: dogs and the army. "Tell the lad, harrumph, to mention my name. Tell him to do that."

Mathilda turned sharply away and, with the Colonel's words still ringing in her ears, made her way rapidly back to the house.

Chapter 16

GASTRONOMIC HIATUS

"What's Mathilda doing out there all this time?" queried Kenneth with a mild lack of interest.

"He's just coming downstairs I think," answered Anne vaguely. She began putting vegetables on various plates.

Kenneth wandered over to the window and looked out at the green lawn where the sparrows and chaffinches, robins and blackbirds, were hopping around feasting off their bread and butter. Further down the garden he could see Mathilda attacking a flower bed.

The sunlight, as it filtered through the intricate network of leafless branches at the top of the trees, transformed the colour of the grass from evergreen to golden green. Kenneth could vividly remember how, long ago, the family used to sit out there during the hot summer afternoons, deep in their bright deck chairs; and he, Kenneth, in his shorts and gym shoes, would play endless table tennis with his father, who must always allow him, after breathless anxiety, to triumph at the end of day.

How well it came back to him: the heavy delicious heat; the faint drone, alternately loud and soft, of an airplane far above; the crack of the spinning table-tennis ball; the fluttering coloured butterflies among the buddleia; and the ladybirds clinging like vivid drops of some strange spotted liquid on the green leaves of the roses; his grandfather sleeping, even then, mouth open, uncomfortably in his chair; the grating of the lawn mower as it was slowly trundled backwards and forwards with studious concentration by North, the gardener; chimes from the church clock at the bottom of the garden – regular, reassuring, musical chimes; and the tea cart wheeled creaking and jolting out to the lawn by a benevolent Miss Tooth. While, from further down the garden, his great-aunt Mathilda's new dog Smith could be heard barking through the summer heat at the vegetables and the traffic which growled back faintly from the invisible road.

Oh there was nowhere like the garden at This'll Do. Nowhere in the world. And the flowers, with their neat inaccurate orange labels, springing up in a wild confusion and to everyone's surprise from where North should not have planted them and could almost swear he had never planted them, were bright and familiar. Flowers never smelled so sweet, nor birds sang so strongly as in that garden.

And the grass, as he minutely examined each slender blade, lying sprawled on the lawn under a low evening sun, was the most brilliant he had ever known. And the sky, as he rolled over on his back and stared up, was the most intense. And where had he ever heard the rustle of an afternoon breeze as it swayed the thick profusion of leaves and stirred them into music equal to that at This'll Do?

But today the trees were bare, the garden grey and cold. And though he might still catch that same aroma of dark earth, of crackling bonfire lit by an older North, of shrubs and fences, wet bark and the old discoloured paving stones, together weaving that peculiar and distinctive essence he knew so well, yet with time the magic gloss grew tarnished, the spell evaporated and was lost. These sudden moments of timelessness, when the past lived again and was real, had become pitifully brief. For all too soon an insidious sense of boredom, of irritation and anxiety, clouded the image, creeping over him like the night.

He was brought back to the present in a rush. Eustace lumbered into the dining room and, without checking his pace or uttering a sound, went lurching out into the garden. Anne began talking but was quickly interrupted by the reappearance of Eustace holding in his hands a bottle of cider.

"What's that?" inquired Anne in a horrified whisper.

The question seemed to confuse Eustace. "What's what?" he demanded uncertainly.

"What's that you're holding?" persisted Anne.

"What?"

"That *bottle.*"

"This bottle, you mean?" asked Eustace still mystified.

"Yes. That bottle of *cider.*"

Eustace regarded it. "It's a bottle of cider."

"*Alcohol,*" breathed Anne. She gave Eustace one of her most emphatic looks.

"I got it in from the garage," explained Eustace. He put the bottle down with a small crash on the table. "It's for Kenneth," he added.

Kenneth mumbled his thanks and began wrestling with the stopper while Anne raised her eyes to the ceiling.

While Kenneth was struggling with the cider, a battle developed in the far corner of the room between Eustace, armed with a knife, and a joint of meat. "What's the damn use of giving me this?" he flared up, flinging the carving knife down with a clatter.

Instead of answering him Anne made a gesture and switched off the lights. They were plunged into unexpected gloom.

"What did you do that for, you fool?" exploded Eustace.

"Can't you see?" Anne innocently asked.

"No. I cannot see!" Eustace was shouting now.

"I see."

"Well, I can't. Be so good as to switch them on at once."

Muttering to herself Anne did so, and Eustace, also muttering, began sharpening the knife.

"I declare unto goodness," suddenly announced Anne, "I don't know what the dickens has gone wrong with my bally feet today."

"Wrong with your belly?" queried Eustace.

Anne took no notice of this obscenity. "Aching like the very devil, they are," she continued. "I keep falling into things: cupboards, hassocks, ottomans. Only Kenneth wants the lamb, Eustace. If there is one thing the child doesn't like, it's brawn, do you, Kenneth?"

"Doesn't like going abroad?" stammered Eustace, advancing from the sideboard knife in hand. "Why, he's no idea – how can he have? Has he ever set foot in Canada for instance? Of course he hasn't. Not yet."

"Brawn, Henry – I mean Kenneth – I'll get it right soon – Eustace!"

"Yes?"

"Brawn."

"No thank you."

"I said *brawn,* not abroad. Kenneth doesn't care for brawn," Anne carried on valiantly.

"You do mumble so, Anne. All the same, Canada's a fine place. That can't be repeated too often."

And now they were sitting at the table.

Kenneth felt glad that Mathilda was in the garden, for that

could only mean they had been too pessimistic over Smith. No-one had said anything about the dog since he had returned from the post office. He did not ask for information. Let sleeping dogs lie, he reflected, without amusement.

In her absence the conversation centred round Mathilda. "She needs a change from this bally hole," Anne explained to Eustace's empty chair as he brushed past her. "A thorough change of air would do her the world of good. We're all bundles of nerves stuck in this place – except Henry of course, who seems to come and go as he pleases. It's just like a boarding house. I'm sick to death of it. When are you thinking of leaving, Miss Tooth – if it's not rude after all these years to ask such a question in my own house."

Mathilda, who had just then entered the kitchen in quest of her lunch, shouted out from halfway within the oven: "I heard that. I have ears, you know."

"You forget how old I am, Mathilda," Anne cried out shrilly. "Come to that," she added quietly, "I can't remember myself."

Mathilda hurried into the dining room; Anne slipped off her chair; and Eustace suddenly came back, sat down, and began eating. He was chuckling ostentatiously over some joke, hoping someone would quiz him before he forgot it.

Mathilda sighed. She knew that Kenneth and sometimes even Henry thought her unfair to Anne. But they did not appreciate what it had been like living with her all this time, hearing that nagging whine of hers ringing in one's ears year after year.

She knew she was as hard as granite with her, but she was not naturally like that – at least she never had been. But Anne took advantage of any sympathy one showed her. If Mathilda did not take a firm line with her she would kill the old man in time. They would all kill one another.

Silence fell round the table. It was not absolute silence – only an absence of speech. As the lunch dragged on, these brief interludes were filled with the steady uproar of Eustace eating. It was a *rattling, clucking, ear-splitting* uproar. This day it was peculiarly noticeable because of Smith's quietness. Usually the dog contributed to the lunchtime orchestra by ravenously swallowing his food under the table, spreading it over their feet, then licking it off.

Perhaps it was because the old man remained so unaware of the disturbance he was creating that Kenneth sometimes ached all over with a longing to tell him about the row he was making. But he never did so, for he knew how he would regret anything he said as soon as Eustace heard it and was hurt. But Mathilda thought differently. Being so deaf himself her brother never noticed that anything was wrong. It was only fair to let the poor man know. Otherwise it would grow into a bad habit. But when she tried to tell him how matters stood and suggest he went to a dentist, it only led to more trouble. She was at her wits' end as how she should handle her brother these days.

As for herself there seemed nothing for it but to eat alone. Meantime she must make sure that he did not forget to phone a vet. She was thinking how best she could do this when Anne began one of her monologues. "Seen anybody you liked better than yourself while you were out this morning?" she suddenly piped up to relieve the monotony. The gravy dripped from the corner of her mouth and Mathilda looked away.

"No – oh yes. I did see Colonel Humblemere on his round of the thicket with Cooper. My word that man is fit with all the exercise he gets. Not like some other people I could name. That's what the army does for a man."

"The army? Christ!" uttered Kenneth.

"There's no need to sneer like that," Mathilda corrected him. "As a matter of fact the Colonel spoke to me. It may interest you to know that the man you are trying so hard to ridicule was concerned with getting your leave extended on compassionate grounds because of Smith's condition."

"Seriously?"

"Of course. He said you might use his name when applying to your Commanding Officer, whoever he may be."

"Oh," said Kenneth weakly. "I didn't know."

Mathilda suddenly let out a loud cry. "Oh God! The birds' lunch. With all the worry over Smith, I quite forgot the birds' lunch. Just listen to them!"

"It's alright," Anne reassured her. "I broke up the bread and handed it to poor Kenneth here who very kindly spread it over the lawn. He did it very nicely, didn't you Kenneth?"

But Mathilda was not appeased by what her sister-in-law said. What bread had she used? How had she cut it up? Anne answered all these questions correctly but not quite convincingly. "What do you take me for – a bally fool?" she protested.

The question was tempting and Mathilda seemed for a moment to hesitate. By an obvious effort of will, she checked herself and continued her cross-examination. Anne swore by every blessed saint she could remember that she had served the birds faithfully and well. But she grew muddled in her answers.

So that day the birds at This'll Do were given a second luncheon.

Chapter 17

P.M.

Once the battle for lunchtime washing-up was over, everyone retired to the solitude of their bedrooms. There, with
the grace of God, they hoped to rob the day of an hour or
two's tedium, emerging refreshed for the evening encounters.
Although Eustace found difficulty in sleeping at night, his main
preoccupation during the day was how to keep awake. Miss
Tooth slept with equal ease day and night. Kenneth found little
difficulty in dropping off in the afternoon. But Anne would
climb the weary steps to her bed and lie in an awkward huddle
praying for oblivion as she waited and went on waiting . . .

She dreaded these lonely afternoons. They succeeded one
another in a dull identical pattern, finding her tormented by
monotony and fearful of the approaching end to her monotony. Perhaps this was why the sight of Miss Tooth lumbering,
with a yawn, up to what she called her "forty winks" irritated her
so much. One could set one's watch by her. Forty winks indeed!
She didn't do herself justice. By the time she condescended to

come down to her tea she would have had ample time for more than forty winks, the old hypocrite.

Eustace had already fallen asleep over his coffee where, after a whispered conference between the women, it had been decided to leave him.

Kenneth had resolved to try and get his leave extended along the lines Mathilda had outlined over lunch. What was there to lose? The Commanding Officer of his battalion, whatever his opinion of human beings, had a sentimental weakness for animals, large quantities of which he often shot at weekends. He might just possibly grant him compassionate leave, especially if Kenneth mentioned Colonel Humblemere's name. It was worth a try. Perhaps he might imply that Smith was his own dog.

But when he telephoned the barracks he was told that the Commanding Officer was out. The adjutant to whom he spoke did not feel justified in committing himself to a decision. Such leave might not be entirely out of the question, but Kenneth must return and submit his request in a letter written in the third-person singular. He would have the opportunity of presenting it at Commanding Officer's Orders the following morning. The matter might be settled then or referred to Brigade Headquarters . . . Kenneth put down the phone with a heavy heart. It was hopeless. He wandered slowly upstairs and lay down on his bed. His suitcase stood ready, packed and waiting for him. All life seemed to consist of waiting. And now he had fewer than three hours to wait.

*

Mrs Gaff, down in the kitchen, eased off her shoes, sat down warmly before the stove, folded her hands comfortably in front of her and closed her eyes. Whether sleeping or waking, an indestructible beaming smile was spread across her face.

Unlike the others, Mathilda had work to get on with. First there was the washing-up again, then the garden once more. After that she must tackle the laundry and a thousand more things urgently calling for her attention. But above all was the problem of the vet. Her face was wrinkled with worry as she battled through her tasks. The sudden ringing of the telephone startled her and, letting go a clatter of knives on to the floor, she raced to answer it. Could it be a vet – someone Eustace had met perhaps while in the village? But a woman's voice answered. It was no-one she knew, no-one the family knew. She shouted out for Mrs Gaff: "It must be for you."

Mrs Gaff came through to the drawing room as fast as she was able, blinking and looking alarmed. Maybe something had happened to her Jonathan. "It must be one of my lovers, Miss Mathilda," she laughed.

"It's some woman. A foreigner, I think. It must be for you," replied Mathilda quickly handing her the telephone.

Mrs Gaff took it and held it at waist level, staring down in perplexity. "Well I don't know I'm sure." She shook her head. Then, raising the receiver very gingerly, and holding it several inches away from her ear, she said: "Yes?"

97

The woman at the other end appeared to speak for a long time, Mrs Gaff every so often mouthing an incredulous word or two. "No . . . I really don't know . . . never heard of it . . . What's that? . . . Missed your toast did you say?"

Mathilda swept impatiently out of the room, and Mrs Gaff was left alone. After a few minutes she lowered the receiver to waist level again. "Must be dotty," she murmured. "Probably the wrong number." Then she spoke into the receiver. "I'm afraid we're all dead here. No-one's at home." Very cautiously, so as not to cause offence, she replaced the receiver.

Kenneth put his head round the door. "Was that Hawkins from battalion?" he inquired. There was a pathetic note in his voice.

"No."

"Not Armstrong?"

"No, Mr Kenneth. It was some woman."

Kenneth was no longer listening, but Mrs Gaff rattled on cheerily. "Do you know what she said? 'Is that Mrs What's-her-name?' She said that three or four times. And 'Can I speak to Mr Thingamy?' As if I'd fall for such a trick!"

Mathilda was watching over Smith. He appeared, if anything, worse this afternoon, and his laboured breathing petrified her. It all seemed so unfair, so unjust. Smith was a dear old boy. Even in his wildest moments, he wouldn't hurt a fly. Why was *he* being made to suffer so? It didn't make sense. If only the vet would come. She braced herself. She would have to do something. Do it now.

As if responding telepathically to this thought, Eustace jolted awake and, noticing Mathilda kneeling beside Smith's divan, made a show of having been awake all the time by noisily drinking up his cold coffee. He never acknowledged falling asleep. At best he would sometime admit to "closing his eyes". But no more. No-one was ever to catch him napping, not if he could help it. He was up to all their tricks. "Oh yes . . . yes I agree," he mumbled, thinking that perhaps Mathilda had said something to him and wishing to be agreeable. With admirable self-control, he stifled a yawn.

Suddenly, with a flash of intuition, Mathilda saw her chance and seized it.

"Yes, you said?"

"I did."

"I'm very grateful to you Eustace. Really I am."

"You are?"

"Yes. I think it's most generous of you to phone the vet at once. And you're right. Smith is not at all himself today, and a second opinion would be useful for us."

"Oh. Yes. Right then."

Mathilda saw she had won. She felt grateful to her brother. "I'm going out now down the village. So I won't be here when you telephone. But I've put a number by the phone. Perhaps you'd keep a special eye on Smith while I'm gone. I'd feel happy to think he was under your care."

"I'll look after the old boy," Eustace agreed hoarsely. With difficulty he resisted an impulse to stretch.

After a final rearrangement of Smith's eiderdown, another smoothing of his blankets, a last prod of his mattress, Mathilda rose to her feet. "Thank you, Eustace," she said again.

Mathilda resented putting on extra clothes when she went out. Dressed as she was, she strode straight out to the garage and began excavating for her bicycle in that great shadowy vault, carpeted with mangy wall-to-wall rugs, where so many of the family's possessions had been buried. Eventually she found it, wheels uppermost, in the recesses of a deep corner where Henry must have flung it. A terrible struggle ensued with sounds of *banging, chattering, smashing* and also *crashing* echoing through the stone-grey twilight.

At last she triumphed and detached the battered vehicle from the wreckage, cursing Henry as she did so. All this trouble was the result of his incurable meddling. He imagined that simply because he had Eustace's permission to keep his car in the garage, he also had the right to shift other people's bicycles (not to mention ladders, suitcases, wardrobes, rocking horses and so on) exactly as he pleased. It was really too inconsiderate of him.

Inside the house Eustace had finally, and reluctantly, made up his mind to telephone the vet. He hated the telephone and had been against installing one in the first place. For some reason people who spoke to him through this instrument always lowered their voices to such an extent that they became unintelligible. The only way to deal with such people was to pay them back in kind. So he would reduce the volume of his own voice until it was barely a whisper. This would excite the person at the other end to greater vocal efforts so that a steady crescendo would build up until both parties were bellowing at each other. The conversation would then progress through an alternating series of whispers and shouts.

The vet whom Eustace phoned that afternoon was no exception to the general run of vets and telephones. Not only did he insist on whispering – and a peculiarly irritating whisper it was – but also, when he shouted, which he did from time to time, he verged on downright rudeness.

Eustace came straight to the point. His sister, he said, wanted to consult him. He had better come round right away – and he could see the dog too while he was about it. That was what he said – or rather what he intended to say. Their dialogue opened conventionally.

"Is that the vet?" the old man whispered.

"Mr Summers here."

"Is that the vet?"

"Yes, this is the vet – Mr Summers."

"I'M PHONING ABOUT OUR ANIMAL."

"OH YES. WHAT ANIMAL?"

"OUR ANIMAL."

"WHAT CAN I DO TO HELP?"

"MATHILDA IS VERY WORRIED ABOUT THE OLD BOY."

"MATHILDA?"

"And Smith does look a bit seedy, I admit."

"Smith?"

"Of course in my view it's merely a matter of . . ."

"What?"

"What?"

"I'm afraid I don't understand you."

"WELL YOU SHOULD, YOU'RE THE VET, AREN'T YOU?"

"THAT'S RIGHT – MR SUMMERS. PLEASE TELL ME WHAT YOU WANT."

"I DON'T WANT ANYTHING, I CAN ASSURE YOU. IT'S MY SISTER. SHE WANTS A SECOND OPINION."

"I THINK I HAD BETTER COME ROUND A LITTLE LATER AND SEE FOR MYSELF."

"THAT'S EXACTLY WHAT I'VE BEEN ASKING YOU TO DO."

"YOU'RE SURE IT'S QUITE NECESSARY FOR ME TO CALL?"

"She thinks so."

"Very well then. What's the address?"

"Farquhar. Eustace Farquhar."

"No. Your address please."

And so the conversation jerked on, Eustace convinced that he was speaking to a man of extraordinary stupidity and the vet also convinced that he was.

Not long afterwards there came the sound of *crashing* and *knocking*, of *banging* and *chattering*. Mathilda had returned from the village with cakes for tea.

Anne rolled awkwardly from her bed and tiptoed downstairs, eager to find out what the noises had been. She put her head into each room but there seemed nothing doing anywhere. Then she shook Mrs Gaff awake and began abusing her. Finally, hearing Mathilda return, she scrambled upstairs again and disappeared into her bedroom. A moment later she emerged carrying a bundle under her arm. Padding across the landing she came to a halt outside Kenneth's room. Here she waited and listened, not knowing what it was she expected or wished to hear. For Anne was convinced that there existed some important secret which she had never discovered, but which was always being discussed behind closed doors and behind her back. She hurried from place to place, from one room to another, in the hope of a revelation that would explain everything.

After a few moments listening at the door, she cried out: "Are you visible, Kenneth?" and began twiddling the handle.

Kenneth was gazing out of the window when his grand-mother entered. He did not trouble to look round as she came in. She began talking to his back. "I've got something for you – a hot-water bottle. It's a proper stone one for the army."

She waited vainly for gratitude. "You'll miss me when I'm dead and gone. Your tea is almost ready." She sighed and gave a shake of her head.

The muffled sound of Mathilda cantering up to her bed-room to wash after being in the village shops, sounded faintly through the door. Anne shuffled further into Kenneth's room which was already growing dark, and continued in a lower tone. "'Poor old granny!' you'll say. 'I wonder where she went. She was a good old thing to me when she was alive, poor soul.'"

"I . . ." hesitated Kenneth. But the next instant a shrill peal from the doorbell downstairs cut him short.

Chapter 18

VERDICT OF ONE

Reactions to the unexpected within This'll Do were complex.
The sudden sounding of a bell could lead to a state of hysterical inactivity that raged on long after its initial cause had
been forgotten.

Mrs Gaff opened her eyes, heaved herself off her chair, and
began stoking the monumental stove as if the bell had rung
somewhere within it.

Eustace also started awake with a twitch and sat swaying on
his lifebelt. He felt almost certain that he had heard the doorbell. But they were not expecting anyone – had not expected
anyone since the end of the war, come to that. There was
no question of opening the door to any Tom, John or Harry.

Mathilda, almost naked in the bathroom, stood absolutely
still. Then with a strangled cry she snatched up a towel and
began rubbing herself vigorously.

Anne raised her hand dramatically to stop Kenneth from
speaking, and then hurried from his room.

The bell rang a second time.

The hysteria gathered momentum.

Anne scuttled sideways down the stairs moaning to herself, while Eustace rose unsteadily to his feet. The two of them met in the hall.

"Did you hear it?" Anne whispered urgently.

"It's the bell," Eustace explained with a brave attempt at appearing in command of the crisis.

"Shh! Keep your voice down. They'll hear you," said Anne, automatically raising her voice.

"It rang twice," Eustace murmured.

"I was up in poor Kenneth's room," Anne replied.

For the next few moments neither of them could think of anything to say.

"Who in heaven's name can it be?" queried Eustace. "At this time of the afternoon."

Anne pondered. "Do you think they'll go away if we keep quiet?"

Eustace favoured more active measures, such as opening a window upstairs and shouting out "Go away!" – words that could hardly be misconstrued. But Anne thought this "not polite". It would be asking for trouble.

Eustace responded by putting his finger to his lips. But keeping silent was more than flesh and blood could stand for Anne. She drew nearer and began plucking at the old man's sleeve. Raising herself on tiptoe, she breathed into his ear: "Do you think they have gone yet?"

For a third time the bell sounded shrilly through the house, longer and more insistent this time, leading to a faint cry from Mathilda, half dressed, upstairs.

Eustace shook his head gravely. "No. I reckon they're still there," he replied.

"Don't answer it," warned Anne.

"My dear woman, I'm not quite so big a fool as I . . . as you make out."

"Only yesterday I read that Lord and Lady Carpet were molested by a gang of ruffians in their own home," Anne went on. "I'd like to flog them all within an inch of their lives . . . I'd . . . I'd like to do more . . . I'd like to spit in their faces! Who do they think they are anyway?" Her voice rose dizzily as she spoke. Then she started scuttling sideways across the hall. Eustace made an unsuccessful lunge to stop her. "You'll be spotted from the window if you don't watch out. They'll go away if only you let them."

Ignoring her husband's advice, Anne beckoned to him. "Here, give me a hand. You're taller than I am."

Reluctantly Eustace moved towards her. Anne's intention was to peep furtively out of the window to spy on the intruders without being seen. Unfortunately, owing partly to the inconvenient shape of the furniture and partly to her lack of height, this presented obstacles. Not the least of these was the initial scrambling on to a small round table the top of which, she knew from previous experience, afforded her a good vantage point. It was to assist with this ascent that she had called Eustace forward. The old man was the least well suited of the family to collaborate in such manoeuvres, but he was the only one who would allow himself to be cajoled into them.

Anne placed her left knee on the rim of the table, at the same time instructing Eustace to catch hold of her right foot and hoist her upwards. He bent down, groped for, and finally grasped hold of Anne's dangling foot. This was the foot on which the old women wore her slipper which, after the first mighty heave, slipped, releasing Eustace backwards on to the floor with a bump while Anne remained where she was, still supporting her weight with one unslippered foot on the floor and the other, in its rubber gardening shoe, on the table.

Sounds of their struggle were communicated to the "intruder" outside who was having some difficulty making sense of them. Anne had somehow attained a position on all fours on top of the table and, by leaning gently forward, could at last draw back the net curtains and peer out. Eustace hovered uncertainly in the background. For nearly half a minute Anne stared intently, then, letting go of the curtains, she turned her head and muttered: "Eustace! It's a MAN!"

As if unable to believe what she had seen, she leaned forward and looked again. "Eustace! He waved!"

Had it not been for all the frenzy and the white face of a wide-eyed old lady at the window, the man might well have left the house for empty. But now he imagined that the bell was not working properly, and began beating out a prolonged tattoo with the knocker.

A door upstairs was flung open, and Mathilda, still struggling into her skirt, let out a terrible cry: "For the love of God will someone open the door? Eustace! Anne! Someone! It must be the vet!"

Pandemonium filled the house. Mathilda continued shouting; Anne chimed in cries; Kenneth added a shout; while Eustace lumbered across the hall and began fiddling with the various latches, bolts and locks of the front door.

"Will you get me off this blooming thing?" wailed Anne.

"For heaven's sake," Eustace shouted back, "give a man a chance, can't you?" He wrenched back the door, but having forgotten to unfasten the last chain, it stuck fast when only a few inches ajar.

"Are you the vet then?" he inquired suspiciously through the slit.

The man outside moved sideways into a position where he could pursue this awkward conversation. "Yes, I'm Mr Summers," he said.

"The vet?"

"Yes, the vet."

"Just a second while I attend to this damned door."

"Right you are."

Eustace slammed the door shut in the vet's face as he spoke, and began meddling with the chain. Mathilda's shouts were still echoing round the walls of the house and Anne, now practically in tears, continued imploring her husband to rescue her from the table top. Then Kenneth made an anxious appearance down the stairs. "It's not Colonel Humblemere, is it?" he asked despairingly. No-one bothered to answer.

The vet had been disconcerted by what he heard outside This'll Do; the bedlam he saw on entering astonished him. For here was an old and stooping man with veined and trembling hands whose bloodshot bewildered eyes stared feebly out of a blood-streaked face; bent too, and haggard, inaudibly mumbling oaths as he urged his guest in and fumbled back the chains and bolts.

And here in the hall was an equally old but tiny white-haired woman whom he had previously spied peering at him through the curtains. But now she crouches astride a small round table, pulling mad faces at him and jabbering like a creature in a circus.

And who is this rushing helter-skelter down the stairs? A tall and panic-stricken middle-aged woman whose once delightful face bears a thousand spidery lines of sorrow and strain; whose clothes are so independently thrown about her bony body; who towers narrowly above them all.

No wonder the vet hesitates.

Eustace is offering his own diagnosis of Smith's condition (a singular lack of chlorophyll "unless I'm much mistaken");

Mathilda, loud in her apologies for the delay, also passes quickly on to Smith, giving a picture of what he had been like as a puppy, his walking feats, the dampness of his nose, the fine way in which he used to wag his tail. And Anne, from her perch a few paces off, extends an elaborate welcome to the MAN, and then, through her persistent cries for aid, persuades the others to help her off the table.

The group moves in procession to the dining room where Smith lies blankly on his bed.

The vet's examination of the dog is distressingly brief. "I'm afraid," he says, "that your dog is seriously ill – very seriously ill." He rose to his feet and went out to the kitchen to wash his hands in the water which, under Mrs Gaff's supervision, was boiling for tea.

"Oh dear!" cried Mathilda. "I *knew* something ought to have been done. I *knew* it."

"Is he going to die?" moaned Anne.

"You're an awful fool!" Eustace cried out in distress. "You've been saying that sort of thing ever since Henry first got the dog. Now do shut up!"

"I only . . ." Anne stopped short on catching sight of the vet coming back into the room.

Eustace sidled towards him, rather embarrassed. "I expect you've had a lot of experience at this sort of thing in your time. So you'll know how things are. My sister is very attached to the dog. We all are."

The two men walked through the hall and stood talking by the front door.

"It's understandable," observed Mr Summers.

"Can we offer you something?" queried Eustace. "Tea or a little cider. Some cakes or cheese?"

"Nothing at all, thank you. I really must be off. I've left your sister some tablets for the dog. He's to have nothing much to eat, plenty to drink. He's seriously ill, you realise, and to be frank he may not last much longer. If any crisis occurs, telephone me at once."

For the first time the reality of the situation forced itself upon the old man's mind. "But is there nothing else we can do?" he asked. "I mean there must be something that would help."

"No, please believe me, there's nothing else at present. Just keep him warm and comfortable. And, of course, the tablets."

With faltering steps Eustace approached the front door, stooped, and began unlocking and unbolting the various burglar devices.

"Goodbye, sir. Sorry I can't be more cheerful." The vet smiled a little uncertainly, walked briskly down the stone path, out through the gate, and into his car.

Eustace stood watching him glumly. Not a bad chap, he supposed. Quite polite. Nothing wrong with him that you could put your finger on. Yet the impression he had left was not wholly favourable. Was it really true that they were so powerless? The old man could not believe it. It was not good enough – not by a long chalk. Vets were often at fault in their diagnoses.

Feeling a tugging at his sleeve, he glanced down and saw that Anne was standing next to him. Mathilda, hands on hips, had also come out.

"Do you know what that traitor's gone and done?" hissed Anne.

Eustace looked at a loss.

Mathilda explained her sister-in-law's words. "Mrs Gaff," she said, "has given us two weeks' notice."

Chapter 19

DEPARTURE

"Kenneth! Kenneth! Your tea's ready. Do hurry up now or you'll miss your train."

Anne's voice, set to music by Mrs Gaff's horn, shocked Kenneth out of a daydream filled with girls. He left his room and went, on weak legs, downstairs.

Seldom had he felt less like eating; never had he seen such a spread laid out before him: sandwiches and toast, chocolate biscuits and cakes, scones with jam and cream. There was enough to satisfy a school. His heart fell.

Anne came bustling up to him. "Are the egg sandwiches alright, Kenneth child?"

"Yes thanks."

"Sure?"

"Positive."

"Enough salt – you can never have too much salt."

"Enough salt."

"What about the Worcester sauce, Kenneth? What about that?"

"That's fine."

"Are you sure everything's alright now?"

"Yes. Everything's still alright."

"Now do buck up," persisted Anne. "Be a comfort to everyone." She looked beseechingly at him, then, moving nearer, plucked at his sleeve. Kenneth edged away. "Alright! Alright! I'm not going to hurt you," she cried, hurt by his reaction. "I expect you'll be glad to get out of this dead-and-alive hole," she went on gloomily. "There's not much to occupy a child in this rotten place now."

Kenneth fingered a chocolate cake apprehensively.

"That's no tea for a growing boy," Anne decided.

Kenneth, trying to swallow, said nothing.

"Not very communicative, are you?"

"Not very," he agreed.

"Oh very well then," she complained, "don't waste your time speaking to your grandmother. She's not worth it. Anyway I'll soon be dead and gone."

Kenneth moved uneasily in his chair.

"Here then, take this. It's two pounds. Come on now, take it. Quickly. And whatever you do, don't let the others know or I'll get into terrible trouble. As it is, they say I spoil you – and that's no more than the truth. Now put it away before anyone comes in. There's a good child."

Kenneth took the money and jumbled it into his pocket as if it were so much waste paper. "Thanks. Thanks very much," he murmured.

Anne talked on, but Kenneth wasn't listening. He was in the grip of a new anxiety. Would the taxi turn up on time? If it was late, he would miss his train and be absent without leave. With his tea hardly touched, he rose shakily from the table.

"But you haven't eaten the cake Mathilda specially got for you," Anne protested.

"I haven't time."

"But it's *Fuller's*," pleaded the old woman.

"I can't! I can't!"

Then, as their combined anxieties rose, the taxi rolled up outside – five minutes early.

Mathilda had not been completely accurate in accusing Mrs Gaff of handing in her final notice. Each year for the past fifteen years the cook had threatened to leave, and each year she was eventually persuaded not to do so. During these tricky periods, Anne was forcibly kept away from her – since it was she whom the others blamed for these crises. All of them lived in terror lest one day she should settle the issue beyond recall.

So regular were these disasters that it is doubtful whether Mrs Gaff ever had any real intention of leaving This'll Do. But she liked to play with the idea. During the week or ten days following her "resignation", she was treated with extraordinary politeness, everyone asking earnestly after her son Jonathan each day. Even North benefited from this atmosphere of clemency to the extent of being called to his face "Mr North", a formality that unnerved him.

When the vet had entered the kitchen to wash his hands, he had remarked, apparently by way of casual conversation and with a jaunty laugh, that it must be rather a tricky job looking after such an eccentric family. That, at any rate, was what Mrs Gaff, still indignant with Anne, had understood him to say above the noise of the tap water. Mr Summers had pointed out that good positions were hard to come by these days – and it was even harder to find good people to fill good positions. Drying his hands, he informed Mrs Gaff that he was on the lookout for someone – a sensible kindly woman to assist him with his work. No special knowledge was required, though it was very interesting work for anyone who liked animals. If Mrs Gaff knew of someone who might like the job of being his office assistant, she must urge that person to call the office for an interview. Early evenings were best.

Then, with a charming smile which seemed to linger in the room after he had gone, he said *au revoir*.

Well, thought Mrs Gaff, she was a kindly sensible woman herself, was she not? He must have been inviting her to apply. So why not do so? These last three weeks with the family had got her down, what with everyone's nerves going to pieces. She would be next on the sick list herself, the rate things were going. Despite all she had done to help out, no-one was the least bit grateful. Mrs Farquhar had been downright rude to her; Miss Farquhar didn't trust her even to do the washing-up; and as for Mr Farquhar, he hardly noticed she was there. Mr Henry, too, seldom noticed her these days, while Mr Kenneth had always been a boy of few words. Even the dog didn't come and sit with her now. What sort of a life was that?

Besides, Mr Summers seemed to be a nice man, a very handsome nice man. Not many of them around these days.

There was no time like the present. She decided to give two weeks' notice at once before she changed her mind. "I'll not be off," she told a speechless Anne, "until that nice Mr Summers has got poor Smith well again. That wouldn't be right. I've never been one to leave folk in the lurch. But in a couple of weeks, once everything is back to normal, I'll be pushing off."

"But where will you be going?"

Mrs Gaff thought it prudent to say nothing as yet. No point in counting your chickens. "You see, madam," she replied airily, "I can't better my lot here. There are no prospects, so to speak. I can't end my days where I am now, can I?"

Anne could make nothing of this. After all Mrs Gaff was one of the family. "Well, I don't know what Mr Farquhar will say, Mrs Gaff, truly I don't. I'm sure he won't be at all pleased."

"I don't know what to say," sighed Eustace after he was told. "What have you done to antagonise the woman now, Anne? You never learn."

"I never so much as opened my mouth!"

"This really is the last straw," said Mathilda flatly. If things came to the worst, she reflected, then North would have to work in the kitchen. She wouldn't have Anne there at any cost, breaking all the glasses and plates.

"Well, I say it's good riddance, the lazy good-for-nothing," shouted out Anne defiantly and hoping that Mrs Gaff would hear her.

"I don't know what on earth Miss Tooth will say," remarked Mathilda. "We'd better not tell her till it's finally settled one way or the other."

Anne snorted in derision; and Eustace shook his head and groaned. Obviously he would have to see Mrs Gaff himself and *speak to her* when the right opportunity presented itself – tomorrow perhaps or the next day. He had done it before, but how he had done it he couldn't remember.

It was a measure of the day's tribulations that no-one thought much of a problem that would normally have preoccupied them to the exclusion of all else. Along the ascending curve of crises and calamities, one calamity more made little difference.

Eustace had been hovering in the hall for twenty minutes. Now, as Kenneth hurried out from his tea, the old man deliberately bumped into him and endeavoured in the darkness to slip a cheque for five pounds into his hand. The cheque fluttered to the ground, both of them dropped to their knees almost sobbing with vexation, everyone gathered round and soon the whole household knew of Eustace's secret gift.

As if by magic they assembled in the hall. Miss Tooth appeared silently from where no-one knew and begged Kenneth not to carry away with him the fine weather predicted on the news. For a moment they fell quiet as Mrs Gaff, all past abuses forgotten, came chuckling out of the kitchen, with a long speech of farewell delivered in one continuous breath, her eyes popping out of her head.

The five of them formed a ring round Kenneth and closed in. "I'm afraid it has been very slow for you here," said Eustace slowly – and he gave a large slow yawn as if to emphasise what he said.

"Oh no. Not at all," Kenneth protested.

"Oh yes it has," insisted Eustace, who disliked being contradicted. "*Very Slow.*" He pronounced these words with such conviction that Kenneth dared not disagree.

"Yes, it's so boring for a child in this blooming hole," agreed Anne like a gramophone record stuck in a groove.

"Oh, I don't know," countered Eustace. "He could do worse for himself than staying here."

Mathilda, black with soot from the boiler and earth from the garden, looked on in silence. Poor old Anne, she thought. Borne out of her own grief, she felt a pang of sympathy for the lost old lady.

Kenneth turned awkwardly to Mathilda. "I hope Smith's alright," he said.

"Thank you."

"Not at all."

There was a layer of unreality over everything. And now the circle closes more tightly and they smile politely. The goodbyes are said and said again in hurried sentences as they stand grouped untidily near the front door. Shuffling around as at a children's party, they extend hands to be shaken, cheeks to be kissed, and all at once no-one can think of anything else to say. No-one except Anne. "Drat it! I've forgotten your carrots, Kenneth."

"But why would I need carrots in the army?"

Everyone was laughing.

"They're very good for you at night – and the nights are bitter now," Anne explained.

At last Kenneth stood alone outside while his luggage was heaved into the taxi. Although the hall door was open, the family had mysteriously disappeared, vanished, every one of them as in a dream. And a wave of unaccountable sadness stole through Kenneth. He walked quickly over to the car. The fumes of the taxi engine rose up in the chill late afternoon air and he began daydreaming. Irritably he shook himself back to the present. It was this confounded daydreaming that made things so difficult.

As mysteriously as they had vanished, the entire family had

now reassembled on the pavement to see the taxi off. They watched him intently as, with clumsy movements, he climbed into the back seat burdened with a heavy overcoat to please his grandmother. Behind him there sounded a chorus of farewells: "*Good luck, Kenneth . . . come back soon . . . don't speak to strangers . . . you'll always find us here . . .*"

From behind the window Kenneth nodded and waved and cleared his throat.

Then, he could hardly believe it, he was finally on his way. Inside the taxi, the driver had switched on the radio, and the bold beat of a brass band raised his departure to an heroic pitch. He twisted his mouth into an ironic indrawn grin and settled back into the corner of his seat, his hands sunk deep into the pockets of his overcoat.

The taxi began laboriously to trundle along the uneven road, its smooth tyres crackling over the gravel and loose chippings. Kenneth turned and gazed back through the rear window at This'll Do receding yard by yard. They were still there, all of them, in an irregular group: his great-aunt in the forefront, her wave like the shake of a fist; his grandmother poised dangerously in the road itself; his grandfather to her left, facing slightly in the wrong direction; Miss Tooth next to him, beaming once more with benevolent short-sightedness; and Mrs Gaff, a yard or so apart, fluttering an enormous blue-spotted handkerchief. A lump rose in his throat as he watched them growing smaller in the distance. He turned back and stared ahead to where a few slender clouds lay stretched out on the horizon.

Soon the taxi drew into the railway station, and a little later Kenneth was standing on the platform waiting for his train. He was almost half an hour too early. A white mist was rising from the ground and hung about the wet branches of the trees. Some lights had been lit, and they wheezed and flickered uncertainly before steadying down to a feeble twinkle, each one the centre of a circle of jumping shadows.

Amid the cold and draughty dampness of the station buildings a few people stood around or wandered aimlessly to and fro. One or two blew misty breath into their cupped hands; others stamped their feet as they waited beside the outlines of their luggage. For the first time that day Kenneth breathed freely. The clutch of anxiety relaxed and his despondency flowed away like an outgoing tide into the night.

All at once bells clanged in the darkness, lights flickered on and off, the signal creaked groaning into position and a lonely voice shouted from far off. The train was hurrying into the station. Soon it began to take shape, seen first by its stream of orange sparks and illuminated smoke, looming along the track through the encircling mist, before it rumbled panting to a standstill.

Kenneth knelt down, picked up his cases and started to stroll along the platform in the gloom. Without difficulty he found an empty compartment, and was hoisting his suitcases into the corridor when a woman's voice behind him cried out urgently: "Hello, Kenneth. Fancy seeing you here!"

He turned and stared through the twilight. "Hello . . ." he answered uncertainly.

"Well, surely you recognise your own mother?" laughed Helga.

Chapter 20

ARRIVAL

Red. Red and amber. Green.

The two cars roared and jumped forward, slowed momentarily as the gears were crashed down, and then shot on again, wheel to wheel.

There was nothing in it. Thirty – forty – fifty miles an hour and still they raced onwards. And now they were streaking round another bend, and then out along the straight line of the road stretching like a dark ribbon into the distance. Cars with glaring headlights surged towards them and were gone; the tall yellow street lights flicked past them faster and faster. Fifty-five – sixty – sixty-five. Neck and neck they went, going hell for leather.

Henry's red round face gleamed and sweated in the evening twilight. He crouched in grim concentration over the wheel. Though he could not be sure, he thought he had just got a nose in front at last. Nothing in it though. He stole a quick glance at the Rover on his right. A more powerful engine perhaps – but what most surprised him was its driver – a *female!* Most women drivers, he knew for a fact, were pests of the first order. But this one certainly knew how to throw her machine around – he'd say that for her.

Green.

Amber.

Red.

The two cars, less than a foot between them, checked their speed – forty – thirty – twenty – and came to a stop alongside each other. The woman in the Rover flashed Henry a smile, revved her engine and waved a hand through the window as if to attract his attention. Henry grinned back like a schoolboy, interpreting these gestures as an incentive for the next lap. He revved his engine terrifically in reply. An attractive piece, he thought, with a striking hairdo, so far as he could make out. Capable, too, unless he was much mistaken. Still, he did not fancy she would get the better of him in the end. With their left hands on the gear levers, right feet pressing impatiently on the accelerators, leaning forward, their bodies tingling with expectancy, they both waited with thumping hearts for the lights to change. But would these infernal lights *never* change? Then just when it seemed they must have stuck permanently, they did change.

Red.

Red and amber.

Green.

Once more, with a whine of engines and a roar of exhausts, they were off. Accelerating and braking, decelerating and declutching, changing up and changing down, skidding and swerving and twisting and turning along the road they whizzed, but Henry could not shake off his rival. The two cars seemed to race along ever-parallel lines at identical speeds.

But now they were approaching yet another set of traffic lights, and Henry began to fall back. Ten – twenty – thirty – yards now separated them and still the gap grew longer. Henry bit his lip and fixed his eyes on the red light ahead. The Rover in front halted, but Henry came on, and then:

Red.

Red and amber.

Green.

He changed into third, pressed his foot hard down on the accelerator, the car bounded forward and he was away. Yes, he had done it. He was past her. She would never catch him now. He grinned to himself, a song rose in his throat and he began humming.

You had to wake up pretty bloody early in the morning to get the better of Henry Farquhar. There were damn few drivers on the road, he could honestly say, who were wily enough to outfox him these days. An old trick that one had been, but she had fallen for it. A fine-looking female though, he thought, with a tinge of sadness.

Pulling up outside This'll Do he glanced at his watch.

Forty-nine minutes flat! At long last he had broken the fifty-minute barrier. Probably just missed Kenneth, though, even if he was earlier than usual. Still, it was a record – no question of that. He would like to see anyone do better.

"It's the hairdo," explained Kenneth. "It makes you look quite different."

"I thought I'd like to have auburn for a change," said his mother. "I had it done this morning. Do you like it?"

"Oh yes, grand. It looks rather mauve in this light. Almost puce."

"They made a mistake. I'm going back tomorrow afternoon."

"What colour is it then?"

"Sort of violet. But listen, I've driven all the way down to see you. What's happened?"

Kenneth looked perplexed and, for a moment, oddly like Eustace. "What d'you mean?"

"I mean that for over two weeks there has been complete silence – no reply to my last letter and no answer to my phone call. Then Romeo tells me you rang with an important message . . ."

"I said *not* important. He's a fool. Look, I'd better get in and open the window."

"And finally," went on Helga, "I ring up This'll Do and some woman tells me there's been an awful disaster – she sounded hysterical."

"Oh that'll be Mrs Gaff, you know, the cook," said Kenneth, clambering into the corridor. He opened a window and Helga told him breathlessly of her day's adventures: how these telephone calls and messages had alarmed her; how, in a panic, she had decided to drive down (she was doing nothing else that day); how she had seen Henry in his car and tried to attract his attention but he had smiled at her and raced off (he was obviously late for an appointment); how she had tried to keep up with him until something had gone wrong with the engine of her car (actually, she remembered, it was her husband's car); and finally, how, having left their car nearby in a garage to be repaired, she had been lucky enough (her only luck so far that day) to come across Kenneth at the station before his train left.

"What did you want to tell me about?" she asked, looking up at Kenneth framed in the train window.

"Only that I couldn't see you this leave, that I'd written to you and forgotten to post the letter and . . . and that's there's nothing to worry about. I'll be seeing you next leave."

"Oh," said Helga. "Oh I see." Her voice trailed off and she stood on the platform at a loss. The guard's whistle shrilled nearby and the engine began steaming noisily. "What'll I do now?" she asked.

"Now you're down here and your car is out of order, you'd

better go along to the house, I suppose. Tell them you've come about the dog."

"The dog?" Helga looked more lost than ever.

"Yes. Smith's very ill."

The train started very slowly to move out into the night. Helga walked along the platform still talking to Kenneth. "But will they want to see me? I mean, won't I be in the way or something? It's been years, you know."

"It'll be alright, I'm sure. They'll probably give you a drink."

Helga's face brightened. "Oh alright then," she said, "if you think I ought to."

The train was now jerking forward more quickly. Helga started to run, then stopped. "Goodbye," she shouted waving a hand. "Glad to have seen you . . . sorry to have missed you."

"Goodbye," called back Kenneth.

They were some thirty yards apart before he remembered the letter. It was still in his pocket. "I say. Wait! I've got that letter for you." He fumbled in his pockets, but by the time he had found it, the train was out of the station, racing along through the bitter blue of the night. "I only hope," he thought apprehensively, "that she doesn't decide to take a coach down to the barracks to collect it."

But Helga was already turning over a visit to This'll Do in her mind. First she should telephone her husband and tell him about his car. Then she would go to have a drink to steady her nerves after all the tedious excitement. And finally she would go up to This'll Do. It would be funny seeing Henry and the others again. Perhaps she might even spend the night there. She would mention the idea to Mr Roach. For some reason the possibility of staying at This'll Do amused her. It would be "nice" talking to Henry after all this time. After all he had been the only *real man* in her life – not counting others.

A mile away in the train, Kenneth had settled into a corner seat and was studying *Bayonet Drill*. All at once the door of his compartment opened and an elderly man with a sword pranced in. "Would you, harrumph, inform me whether this seat is taken?" he politely asked. Kenneth indicated that it was not taken. The old soldier sat down and appeared to study Kenneth intently. Then, apropos of nothing, he announced: "Even after quarter of a century, a man must, hmm, break out in an emergency."

Henry was already in mid-sentence as he came through the front door, so there was no opportunity to tell him about Smith.

"Had a terrific tussle on the way here with a Rover," he declared.

"Henry . . ." began Eustace, but got no further.

"Showed her a clean pair of heels in the end though."

"Henry . . ." pleaded Mathilda urgently.

"Managed to clip a couple of minutes off the old record."

Miss Tooth made a noise at the back of her throat.

"Female, too, which took me back I can tell you. There can't be many who drive like that."

"Kenneth – I mean, Henry . . ." shouted Anne.

"Old Harris agrees with me," persisted Henry, preparing to deliver his monumental piece of news. "He's nobody's fool. D'you know, he's actually settled the merger I was telling you about."

And now at last that Henry paused to observe the effect of his news, there was absolute silence. "Ah," he resumed, "I knew you'd be surprised."

Eustace, whose truss was hurting him, started to limp off upstairs to his bedroom where he could adjust it in private. But Henry, slapping an arm round his shoulder, overtook him in the hall and held him there talking optimistically about the future of celluloid and mergers.

"Some people are really *too* bad," Mathilda cried out suddenly. She stalked out to the garage, took off the handbrake of Henry's wretched car and pushed it halfway outside. Then, grabbing hold of her bicycle from the top of a wardrobe where Henry had flung it again, she placed it reverently, centre-stage, on some carpets in the middle of the floor. That would teach him!

A sound of *knocking*, of *clattering* and *banging* reverberated through the house and broke into Henry's monologue. He paused, mouth open, one hand raised – and Eustace, quick to spot his opportunity, made off upstairs.

Left alone, Henry let out a weary sigh and dropped into the nearest armchair with a loud explosion. He felt despondent. For all he could see, he might as well have been addressing the back end of a bus. Mathilda, he sometimes thought, was the worst offender. Occasionally he even wondered whether he had done the right thing by giving her Smith all those years ago. But then women were so damned unpredictable. One never knew what to do for the best. But here she was now, hot from the garage. He would try to reason with her. He cleared his throat. "Mathilda," his voice rumbled forth from the depth of his armchair as his aunt dashed around him dusting, tidying, sweeping. "Mathilda, if you'll permit me for a second to make one simple observation, I've had occasion to notice that you've no system to your routine. . ."

Mathilda said nothing, but began hitting the furniture and cushions and carpets. Bang! . . . Bang! . . . Bang!

". . . I mean, if only you made a business plan or something of the sort and got it down perhaps on paper one evening – I'd assist you with that of course – then I believe you'd get through twice as much in half, shall we say, the time."

Bang! Bang! Bang!

Henry shifted uncomfortably in his chair. "A small thing, I grant you," he persevered, his voice oozing reasonableness, "but take for example the way you lock and bolt the garage doors and put your bicycle in the way before I arrive back in my car of an evening. Just take this single incident, I say, trivial though it may strike you in itself. Now, not to mention the irritation it causes me – I repeat, not to mention this at all – you are creating quite unnecessary trouble for yourself. It's a small item, I daresay, but it does serve to illustrate – rather neatly I think you'll agree – your basic flaw."

Bang! Bang! Bang!

"Little things like this, or the way you stow away my overcoat the very second it leaves my back so that it cannot be found again for several days afterwards (days which, as often as not, turn out to be quite the coldest in the whole damn year); the way you always steal away the hose and bury it in the garden so that my car looks as if it had recently emerged from a coal mine . . ."

BANG! BANG! BANG!

Dust and violent noise were rising all around Henry as Mathilda laid into the furniture with the ferocity of a hurricane. But Henry had got into his stride, and raising his voice to compete with the accelerating rumpus, his face growing coloured with the exertion, his brought his speech valiantly to a conclusion: ". . . all these seemingly petty things, Mathilda, and countless others besides, trivial in themselves I don't deny, take a great deal out of you and, not to mince matters, out of the rest of us also. Now I don't wish to appear unduly critical – nothing could be further from my intentions – but without some system, some efficiency agenda, you're in the bloody soup."

As Henry ceased speaking, so the noise about him abated, the dust settled, and there facing him, hands on hips, stood Mathilda. She opened her mouth to tell him something. But suddenly the futility of it all swept over her and she came out with something else. "Poor Smith is very seriously ill, you should know. We've had the vet in. He said that Smith may die."

Henry jerked forward in his chair. "By Jove, Mathilda, I am sorry to hear that," he said, genuinely moved. "I know how much the old boy means to you."

But the words of consolation had come too late, and already Mathilda was hurrying off elsewhere.

Alone again, Henry pondered heavily. After the long-awaited triumph of the merger that he could share with no-one, after the thrills of the drive that no-one wanted to hear, a great weariness overcame him. He could not continue with this kind of life for ever. His dream was to save up enough money to buy a cottage somewhere in the country (nothing too grand), to marry again (he didn't deny it), not to some silly little bit of a girl who never knew her own mind but to an attractive mature woman (like the mother he never had) – someone who could cook too! His mind drifted back to the driver of the Rover.

Henry didn't ask for Heaven any longer. Thirty-odd years of disappointment in the aftermath of two world wars had once and for all put paid to that dream. But he did want a real home of his own, a place where Kenneth could come and go as he pleased, and a wife – that he supposed was necessary. He couldn't always be on his own. Surely that was not too much to ask from the world.

Sometimes, in the evenings, when he was tired and the racket in the house was at its loudest, it seemed to him that anywhere else would be preferable to carrying on as he was doing now. Simply anything. It got so damned lonely there day after day, you wouldn't believe it. He was a foreigner in his own family.

But this would never do. Rousing himself, Henry got up from his chair and glanced at his watch. Time, he fancied, for a bath.

Chapter 21

BOILER, BATH AND PIPE

Because of the problem of hot water, baths were discouraged at This'll Do. As Anne had once or twice remarked of Helga who, if you please, insisted on having a bath every day: "Some people must be very dirty indeed to need that amount of washing."

At the back of the house, and invading the edge of the lawn, stood the great shed that housed the boiler. Since This'll Do was heated solely by oil, and all the cooking was done by electricity (the gas oven being used primarily for the storage of old newspapers and the stove for the boiling of water for tea), the sole function of this massive boiler house was to provide the family with, as the advertisement had put it, "a constant stream of scalding water night and day".

Eustace, besides having paid large amounts of money for the various heaters that were scattered dangerously around the rooms and buried away in the garage, had also "forked out a small fortune" installing this hot-water unit and, subsequently, in purchasing many tons of the highest-grade coal and new smokeless Bronowski Bricks with which to feed it.

Eustace, together with Mathilda, occasionally Mrs Gaff, and, when she imagined no-one was looking, Anne herself, tended it one after the other day and night. But this dark monster, standing huge and pitiless above them, seemed, as if in a fairy story, to have fallen asleep. For the ultimate product of all their exertions was a meagre amount of warm or tepid water barely sufficient for the innumerable washing-up sessions.

The person who attracted the greatest weight of censure for this steady inadequacy was North. He came one day a week, ostensibly to look after the garden, but in reality to serve as the target towards which all the family's mistakes of the previous six days could be aimed. On the evenings of the Thursdays on which he came, the family having worked off all its collective grievances on him, he magically emerged as "a good fellow" as Eustace habitually called him. "You don't come across his sort often these days," he would declare, summing up the feeling of them all.

But as the days passed, North appeared in a less and less favourable light until, by the following Wednesday, Eustace, again giving expression to a unanimous feeling throughout the house, would denounce his absent gardener as "a damn fool and no mistake!"

In spite of all this, North enjoyed his time at This'll Do and was always offering to come along whenever he was needed.

For despite the changeable climate of opinion, Eustace was genuinely fond of his gardener who, bombs or no bombs, had loyally come through the war in their garden.

North had been approximately the age of forty-five for as long as anyone could remember. He had pale watery eyes that were almost invisible, sparse fair hair, and a permanently open or puzzled expression depending on the day of the week and the time of the day. He was physically rather weak, but always eager to do anything he was asked to do (no-one ever *told* North what to do).

When he arrived on Thursday mornings, looking vacant, he would either employ himself shifting his weight from one foot to the other (which meant that no-one had given him any clues as to what he might do) or else performing some peculiar operation with a quizzical expression on his face (such as riding his bicycle round the lawn with the hose playing over the wobbling handlebars) which meant that a number of people had given him contradictory or incomprehensible suggestions for the day. His mind grappling to assimilate them, he would give his watery smile and manage as best he was able.

The one place he never went to was the shed that housed the boiler. The chief contestants there, wrestling for the obscure privilege of stoking this infernal machine, were Eustace (who claimed that no-one else really understood how to operate it) and Mathilda (who believed that Eustace was not in a fit enough state of health to take on such a heavy responsibility). Compared with the battle between these two chief adversaries, the haphazard skirmishes of Anne and Mrs Gaff were trivial affairs that did little harm. Great arguments would circulate round the house about "the problem of hot water" and plots of infinite cunning and resourcefulness were hatched out in secret by various antagonists. Mrs Gaff, when she got the opportunity, fed it on a diet of old rags; Anne helped it to plenty of over-ripe fruit; Eustace used old and sometimes, inadvertently, current newspapers; Mathilda carried armfuls of leaves and sticks to it from the garden. All these were by way of being appetising titbits added to the regular diet of vintage coal and Bronowski Bricks. The resulting indigestion was incurable.

Despite all the family could do, and threatened to do, Henry stubbornly persisted in enjoying "a good bath" unaware apparently that his enjoyment gave rise to much disarray. It was his habit to accompany the sounds of innocent splashing with a ballad or two rendered in his penetrating bass voice which conveniently kept out the sounds of distress. Ten minutes after rising from his chair there could be heard against the fierce agitation of the water a lusty version of "Maid of the Mountains".

Henry's "goings-on", as she called them, infuriated Mathilda. Soon she was storming round and round the landing, up and down the stairs, and glaring at the bathroom door through which the concerts of water-music, the splashing and the singing, were escaping. "Really, it's disgraceful of Henry," she expostulated as she strode through the house. "He's already used up tomorrow's water – and now he's turned on the tap again. He's using every single drop!" Driven almost frantic she rushed downstairs and into the dark garden and the darker shed, hoping Henry could hear her through the window.

Anne, meanwhile, was employing different tactics. Every three minutes or so she approached the bathroom and, like a police officer, knocked loudly on the door. She then rattled the handle and opened the door ajar, shielding her eyes and shouting out through the volumes of steam and general uproar: "Are you alright in there? You're not drowning, are you? If you stay there any longer you'll ruin the pores of your skin."

While this was going on, Eustace was holding court in the dining room, explaining with his customary optimism the technology of hot water supply to an all-attentive Miss Tooth. "You see," he told her, "it's not as if we don't have hot water. We've got as much as anyone could possibly want – enough to float a battalion. I wonder if you understand that, Miss Tooth."

Miss Tooth nodded energetically. She knew it by heart.

But the old man wanted to make sure. "All we need is a little notice beforehand. A day would do – or two days even better. Then everything would be as easy as falling off a log. If only Henry had come and had a quiet word with me yesterday, or preferably the day before, I could have managed it in a jiffy. Fetch me a pencil and I'll show you."

A pencil was produced.

"And some paper."

Paper appeared.

"Now the boiler works like this . . ." And with a number of shaky lines, Eustace began his lesson on boiler drill.

By the time Henry had emerged, still crooning, from the bathroom and gone to dress in his bedroom, the upstairs party had joined the downstairs party in a council of war.

"This sort of thing cannot be allowed to continue indefinitely," fulminated Mathilda. "Eustace, you will have to *speak to him*."

"Do you think it's safe, Eustace?" Anne inquired with a tremble in her voice. "It won't blow up or anything with all the extra work Henry is giving it?"

And from Miss Tooth, treading the tightrope of family diplomacy, there came discreet coughs, ambiguous sighs and furtive nods of her head.

Into this conflagration of family emotions Henry soon entered, bathed, refreshed and humming to himself. But he knew something was wrong. Faint sounds of desperation had penetrated the scrubbing of his feet, neck and moustache, and the yodelling of "Maid in the Mountains". As he thoughtfully dried himself, he was forced to realise from the dull thunder of the conclave below that, somehow or other, he had been the cause of dismay.

As he walked into the room, adopting a self-protective

swagger, silence descended. A deep heavy saturated silence it was, steeped in hostility. Four pairs of indignant eyes turned accusingly to the culprit, while Henry began apprehensively tinkering with his pipe. Then, to everyone's consternation, Anne spoke: "Really Eustace, I agree with you. We'll have to move. Perhaps, as you say, we should live in the garage for the rest of our lives. It's either that or a hotel. I'll start packing now – we can't cope here anymore."

Eustace of course had not said anything of the sort. He was confused by Anne's remark and, preferring to speak of other people's shortcomings in their absence so as to avoid "unnecessary unpleasantness", he remained silent. On the appearance of Henry, he shut his eyes and let all thoughts of the boiler vanish. Mathilda's fury too suddenly switched from Henry towards Anne.

"Why don't you all arrange to have me shot at dawn?" Henry suggested mildly. He did not realise that the storm had swept past him. In any event, his mind was moving to a simpler subject. He wanted to smoke. Despite many painful scenes in the past, he could not see how "smoking a simple pipe" could harm anyone. And so now, as he took out his pipe and began knocking it ominously against the mantelpiece, table and window sills, a fresh wave of indignation arose from the rest of them.

Unperturbed, Henry began the complicated business of lighting his dormant pipe. It took him ten minutes to get it satisfactorily lit. There he stood sucking and inhaling as if his life depended upon it, his feet gradually disappearing beneath whole boxes of matches. Then all at once, as from some Indian encampment, a cloud of dense smoke ascended impressively into the air, announcing that the first stage had been completed.

A groan went up from the family.

Next, sitting deeply back in his chair with a grunt of approval, Henry started upon the process of actual smoking. This involved much puffing and deep breathing, while from the pipe itself there came a series of insidious sucking noises as if it were being used by a child for blowing bubbles. Despite this, within a minute or two it had gone out, and Henry, displaying his stamina to the full, prepared to start from the beginning once more.

This was the pattern of smoking that Henry employed over the next half hour, a pattern broken every so often by a tremendous burst of coughing that seemed to take him (if no-one else) utterly by surprise. Four times during this half hour he was overtaken by such a paroxysm. As he staggered blindly around the room, his body wracked and twisted by violent spasms, his eyes streaming from the thick black smoke that issued from the chimney of his pipe (which he still held with unconscious tenacity between clenched teeth), he blew myriad sparks and a snowstorm of tobacco flakes through the air for a remarkable distance, scattering his relations. After each successive seizure, he sank exhausted into the chair again, muttering weakly about something "having gone down the wrong way".

"I hope to God Kenneth never wastes his money on smoking," Anne cried out through the swirling fumes.

"It's a perfectly disgusting habit," agreed Mathilda, who kept running in and out of the room to avoid the fetid atmosphere.

A loud snore from Eustace sounded in response to her statement. The lack of oxygen had got the better of him.

At last it became too much for Mathilda. Binding a handkerchief around her nose and mouth, she began opening all the windows. In little over a minute the room was empty. She closed the windows, sat down beside Smith's divan, and began whistling softly to the unconscious dog, tenderly ruffling his fur with her fingertips. She felt sad but was at peace.

Chapter 22

REMOTE CONTROL

Five minutes after being evicted from the dining room, the family were widely dispersed through the house.

Mathilda, back in the kitchen, was hustling Mrs Gaff out of the back door so that she could rewash the washing-up with what drops of water remained. "Cheerio! Cheerio! Hope you're all alive in the morning!" shouted Mrs Gaff, unabashed by her recent treachery. She would have stopped longer and said more had not Mathilda given her a polite push and slammed the door behind her.

Anne, who had meanwhile sneaked back into the dining room, was laying the table for supper and, simultaneously, for the next day's breakfast and lunch, moaning to herself in the darkness as she juggled with sets of knives, forks and spoons.

Eustace had retired into the withdrawing room where, deep in meditation, he covered the backs of unopened envelopes with complicated figures.

Miss Tooth wandered upstairs to her spic-and-span cupboard.

And Henry had plunged into an armchair in the hall, where he sat contemplating the evening paper.

This distribution of the household through a series of rooms, one of them upstairs, in no way hindered their powers of conversation. By raising their voices to a satisfactory level (approximately double the normal volume) it had been found that results could be obtained identical to those produced when they were herded together in the same room. It was quite possible to broadcast a perfectly respectable quarrel without anyone moving at all.

It began from the direction of the kitchen from where a voice shrilled: "Eustace! We'll miss the weather if we don't watch out."

"Alright! Alright!" another voice answered from the drawing room.

"Dear me!" sounded the hall. "What a tragedy *that* would be!"

"There's no need for that," protested the drawing room.

"She needs a holiday," moaned the dining room.

"Ha!" exclaimed an upstairs cupboard softly.

"The television. Please!"

"Oh alright. I'm just doing it now."

Still no-one moved.

"Can you remember how it's done?" anxiously inquired the dining room.

There was a sharp intake of breath in the drawing room. To be subjected to such a question now after so many weeks gaining valuable experience at the controls! "Yes, of course I do. Any child . . ."

"Why hasn't it come on then?"

A switch clicked and after a moment of silence the whole house was filled with a deafening volume of noise, a *crackling* and *burring* and *whistling*.

"Give me a minute, for pity's sake," the drawing room called out.

The beat of a light Cossack dance took over from the initial barrage of sound and wafted through the rooms, punctuated by a fresh cry from the dining room. "Would you like Henry to see to it for you, Eustace? I'm sure he wouldn't mind." The trouble with Eustace, thought the dining room, was that he had never regained his confidence after blowing out all the lights in the street with one of his experiments a few months back.

"Yes of course I'll do it," boomed the hall. "Nothing simpler. Would you like me to lend you a hand, pa?"

"No I would not! I'd take it very kindly if you'd all mind your own business for a change."

There arose a chorus of recrimination, some of which, it being a Tuesday, fell on North.

"Is the bally thing broken?" wailed the dining room with eager pessimism.

"It's just coming on now. Sh!"

"Sh!" echoed the upstairs cupboard.

"Sh!" repeated the hall and kitchen.

"One daren't open one's lips in this blooming house," complained the dining room.

"Shhh!" let out the other rooms.

As the first intelligible words issued from the television, a strange and terrible spell seemed to fall upon the family. The wireless had acted as a catalyst on their feelings, but the television became a powerful magnet pulling everyone to it. Like sliding tentacles of noise, the throbbing sentences crept through the house, insinuating themselves into each separate room to coil around its occupant and pull him, pull her, back. As men and women who have simultaneously lost their willpower to a sinister hypnosis, they were dragged, helpless and unprotesting, down and across to the drawing room where the old man sat unblinking as he fumbled with the controls of this new, magical machine. They moved like somnambulists in some collective nightmare; like prisoners who have been condemned to live out their lives in a sunless dungeon, but whose sentence permits them to stare each evening for a few hours through a keyhole at the incomprehensible world outside.

"Good evening," said the announcer, appearing suddenly before them on the screen.

Their friend was back. "Good evening," returned the family.

Eustace straightened his tie, Mathilda nodded, Anne smiled. A distinguished personality had entered the house.

Eustace watched the news for any allusion, however coded or oblique, to corned beef; Henry, for any derogatory remarks about pop groups – he liked to sigh and jeer at their lazy, asymmetrical appearance. Mathilda, more exhausted than she realised or liked to admit, would usually drop off into a troubled sleep as soon as the television came alive – though it was she who was most adamant about not missing the news. Sometimes she would talk during these fits of sleeping, sometimes as if speaking to Smith but mostly repeating words of invective and abuse.

For Anne the most striking information was the weather. It affected her profoundly, travelling to her feet, but also making excursions to other regions of her body – her head, her back and her knees. The weather also played havoc with her appetite, her bunions and bones. When the northwest part of the country entered a low trough, Anne immediately felt low herself. When the atmosphere was high, her blood pressure rose. She was always on the lookout for lightning which she was certain would one day strike her dead, and at the first suspicion of a storm she would disconnect the lights, hiding away the bulbs, and hurry into the garage for protection. She regretted that North had filled in the air-raid shelter that had lain under the vegetables in the garden – she had felt safe there even from Hitler. As it was, rain seldom failed to give her flu and the sun laid her out or gave her a rash. She was a martyr to the weather, Anne.

Miss Tooth, whatever the programme, watched it intently at about twelve inches from the screen. Seldom did a movement, a gesture, however small, escape her. She heard every word, every syllable that was uttered, but had difficulty connecting these sounds with the pictures and gaining much understanding of what was going on. Nevertheless, she sat undisturbed in front of it for hours in the darkness.

Henry, who was strongly addicted to the television, objected in principle to much of what he saw, partly because the others chose programmes he didn't like. Eustace maintained that since they had gone to the expense of installing this contraption, it was best not to risk missing anything. And how was one to guess what was worth watching without trial and error? "Well, it may not be too bad," he often said. "You never know. It doesn't hurt to give it a chance. Besides these programmes sometimes have a habit of warming up as they go along." To be on the safe side, he kept switching programmes "just in case". Miss Tooth seldom noticed these changes, but Henry, who had difficulty seeing past her and was unable to keep up with Eustace's rapid changes, would leave the room in exasperation.

Anne's opinion of the television varied according to which

room she was in. When she was in the kitchen or scullery, it was "a blooming nuisance", but when she reached the drawing room it became "a pure godsend". So far as the others were concerned, it was difficult to decide which was the more disturbing. For some reason Anne particularly relished the trailers. "People are so clever nowadays. There's nothing they can't do. Why don't you go and win yourself a fortune, Henry? Go and answer some of those questions they ask instead of sitting on your *derrière*. I'm sure Kenneth could do it if he tried."

"Quiet!" hissed Mathilda who had just then woken up. "Oh dear, the thriller is starting."

Anne was bemused by thrillers but whenever the villain appeared she would screech "swine!" or "lout!" or "coward!" Then suddenly she would rush hobbling out to the kitchen shouting "The pies! The pies!", reappearing after a few minutes with a query: "Would you like your supper now, Eustace?", raising her voice over a cacophony of galloping hooves and pistol shots. It was not a thriller but the cowboys.

"Not yet," retorted the old man. "I'm watching this programme."

"It's only Anne making a nuisance of herself as usual," explained Mathilda.

Henry glanced across at Anne who at that moment had wandered directly in front of the screen, blocking everyone's view. In a voice as stern as doom and loud as a band he barked out: "Go and sit down and watch the bloody show, mother. And for the love of mike, keep quiet. You're causing chaos!"

Anne stood there waving her arms.

"Oh alright, alright," sighed Eustace. "You win. We'll eat now and have done with it, if that'll satisfy you." And suddenly, unthinkingly, he switched off the television.

"It's always the way," groaned Anne. "Never a word of warning."

Through the darkness Miss Tooth blinked twice in silent disappointment.

Chapter 23

LAST SUPPER

Since Mathilda thought it unhealthy to eat at night and Miss Tooth absented herself in sympathy with Mathilda, only the other three went into the dining room.

"Eustace," inquired Anne, "would you like one of those pies or a little cold ham?"

"The ham, I think," answered Eustace.

"The pies are very good."

"Alright then, I'll have a pie."

"You can have either."

"I don't mind which I have. I really don't mind."

"Well, they're both there, you know."

Eustace looked badgered, as if he were being obliged to eat something he didn't like. "Anything you say, Anne," he pleaded.

"It's entirely up to you," Anne persisted. "They were both bought for eating. I don't want to force you to have anything."

"Very well then, I'll have nothing."

"Now don't be silly."

"For pity's sake just give me something – anything."

"You're becoming very difficult to please, Eustace. Very difficult. Not at all like Kenneth. I do hope to goodness he's alright. What do you think, Henry?"

"One of the pies for me please, ma."

"No, I mean about the poor child in the army. Will they ever feed him properly, I sometimes wonder."

"Hardly ever, I should say."

"Oh Henry! Really?"

"Don't be so silly, ma," Henry relented with a chuckle. "Of course he'll be alright. He's only got six months more to get through. It's the same for everyone, you know."

"I'm not worried to death over everyone."

Since the conversation gave no sign of coming to an end, Eustace decided to break into it. "If we don't get a move on, Anne, those pies of yours will be stone cold."

"Oh but Eustace," the old woman answered in surprise, " I thought it was the ham you wanted."

No sooner had one of the pies been put before him than Eustace, much to Anne's chagrin, got up and stumbled out of the room. Nor was she best pleased when, five minutes later, he returned to a plate of cold ham with a bottle of cider. Eustace knew that Henry "liked something" in the evening and, feeling perhaps that he had not shown adequate enthusiasm for his son's business news, whatever it was, he now presented this bottle to the table to mark the occasion. Henry beamed. "You really shouldn't have," he said to the old man, taking the bottle from him and vigorously twisting open the top.

"Fire water!" breathed Anne.

Henry glanced round at her and then, giving Eustace a broad wink which the old man failed to notice, he asked: "Would you like some, mother?"

Anne shivered and shook her head.

"Come off it, mother," Henry went on with a great braying laugh which sent shooting pains thought Anne's head, while Eustace joined in uncertainly. "Come off it. There's no harm in cider, or even wines in moderation," Henry continued. "As I often tell Kenneth, be careful with the spirits – they'll ruin your sport. But wines are quite a different kettle of fish."

Anne raised her eyes to the ceiling. "Teaching the child to drink! Whatever next?"

Henry drank deeply and sat back.

Meanwhile Eustace was volunteering something about his truss which, despite various readjustments, was giving him pain again. As he was drawing a diagram to help Anne understand the problem, Mathilda came in. For a moment she looked across at them all eating, drinking and squabbling. The fact that they were able to enjoy their supper while Smith was so desperately ill and could not eat enraged her. At times she loathed them all, what with their drinking and their snoring, their pipes and silly talk. She watched them without saying a word, then crossed the room and knelt down beside Smith's divan.

In the next moment she uttered a scream. "Eustace!" she cried. "I think . . . I think Smith's stopped breathing."

Chapter 24

SUSPENSE

The three of them rose to their feet.

"He *can't* have!" exclaimed Eustace. "We've been here all the time."

"Not like *that*," protested Henry. "I thought he was getting better."

"I knew it." Anne had no doubts.

They clustered round the divan. Smith was still breathing, but the rise and fall of his breath was barely perceptible.

"Thank God!" said Mathilda. A great tiredness came over her. "Silly of me. He was always a gentle breather."

"You gave us all a shock there, old girl," said Henry gruffly, and blew into his hands. For all his apparent robustness, Henry hated the sight of pain.

The others now closed in on Smith with anxious expressions, and Miss Tooth joined them from the hall where she had been waiting for the television to show pictures again.

"You'd better phone the vet before it's too late," volunteered

Anne, turning towards her husband.

"Leave it to me," interrupted Henry. "I'll phone him right away." He hurried out of the room.

While they waited, the three women and Eustace sat down near Smith. Mathilda yawned. In spite of herself her eyes kept closing and her head sank forward as if pressed down by a heavy weight. Miss Tooth mouthed quiet words of comfort as if to a child. Anne sat with her head in her hands murmuring the names of the saints. Eustace frowned, not knowing what to do.

Then Henry came back. "The vet says he'll be up here very shortly," he reported. "In about twenty minutes or half an hour. We're to do nothing until he comes."

No-one spoke. Henry coughed. "I'm popping out. Won't be a minute," he said. "Just off to get some tobacco." He hurried out of the room.

"You know where he's gone, don't you?" demanded Anne. "To the public house, of course."

Bewildered and dismayed by Smith's condition, the family relieved their feelings by criticising Henry.

"I'm surprised he hasn't more decency," Anne continued. "Where he gets it from I don't know. Neither his father nor myself would have been seen dead in such a den. Not for the life of us."

"Really," said Mathilda weakly, and jerked her head upright.

"Mathilda's the most abstemious person I know," Anne

went on. "She's a fine example to others I could name."

Mathilda stretched. "Really, Anne. Really."

"There's nothing worse than drink in this whole rotten world," persisted Anne. "All the dregs of the universe are to be found in those pubs, they tell me. If I had my way they'd be put in prison – and that's too good for them." Her voice was so vibrant with emotion that she astonished herself. She didn't really care about drinking in pubs. She simply felt the need to talk, to object.

"I understand that they're often unclean places," said Mathilda, surprised to hear herself joining in the conversation.

"If he wanted a drink he could easily have got one here – in the garage," pointed out Eustace.

"He's had plenty already," added Anne, pointing to the half-empty bottle of cider.

Mathilda screwed up her face but said nothing.

"It's my belief," Anne continued recklessly, "that all this trouble in the world is the way they allow them to breed – like rabbits they are."

She was prevented from embroidering this line of argument by the reappearance of Henry who was welcomed back with relief. He went to Smith and, making up for his absence, began patting and speaking to him. The rest of them grouped round expectantly. "Must say the poor blighter does look a trifle under the weather," was his verdict. The group broke up and returned in silence to their places, sitting down at the table as if for another meal. Henry took out his pipe, knocked it experimentally in the palm of his hand, and placed it back in his pocket. No-one spoke.

There sounded an uneven tapping at the front door.

"It's the vet!" cried Mathilda and, before anyone had time to move, she had dashed off to the door, like a sprinter jumping the gun. The others, suddenly shy and diffident, stood waiting for her return. They heard her tearing at the bolts and chain, opening the door and saying: "Oh, it's you of all people! You must have come about Smith, I expect. Do come in – we're all in the dining room."

A moment later the door opened again and in tripped Helga, giggling nervously.

After telephoning London to tell her husband she was stranded but safe, Helga had set off for the White Rabbit, a pub near This'll Do, where, in the bright warm saloon hazy with cigarette smoke she felt at home with a large glass of whisky in her hand. She was soon deep in shallow conversations with strangers who offered her more drinks and whose company produced an odd reluctance to complete her journey. To help her on the way she ordered some sandwiches and a final drink "for the road". But when she finally left she took the wrong road and narrowly missed Henry making for the pub. Half an hour of roving the streets did much to clear her head.

After ringing the bell and while waiting for the front door to be prised open she recalled Kenneth's advice and decided to announce that she had come to see Smith, however unlikely it sounded to her own ears. She was all the more taken aback when Mathilda, flinging open the door and recognising her at once, took the words out of her mouth as it were: "Oh, it's you of all people! You must have come about Smith. Do come in."

She obediently agreed and, taking off her coat, was led into the dining room where the family was preparing to welcome the vet. Everyone was astonished. Despite the vivid colour of her hair and the years that had elapsed since their last meeting, both Anne and Miss Tooth recognised her immediately. And both were delighted: Anne because of the fresh excitement she brought; Miss Tooth because in the past Helga had been scrupulously polite to the old woman of whom she was always a little afraid.

To Eustace it was a complete stranger he saw before him. But Henry was the most surprised of all, recognising at once the driver of the Rover earlier that day, and only subsequently and with a medley of emotions his ex-wife. Before anyone could express amazement, Mathilda casually explained: "Helga's very kindly come along to find out about poor Smith." After which everything seemed quite natural.

"Kenneth must have told you all about it," said Anne. "He

left for the army this afternoon, poor mite. Pity you missed him – he might have liked seeing you. Still, it's certainly a change to see a new face about the place, even an old one. Now tell me, what time are you leaving?" Her words, however tactless and abrupt, had no malice in them and no-one took any notice of her.

Miss Tooth calculated that it must be the best part of a dozen years since they had last shaken hands. Then, having no other way of showing her goodwill, offered her a nice cup of tea – which Helga firmly declined.

Eustace, meanwhile, peered at her and shook his head.

"Well, I'll be buggered," burst out Henry, lunging forward and grasping hold of Helga's arm. "Excuse my French. But really, old girl, I never recognised you. Must be the hair."

Helga felt rather irritated by yet another reference to her hair. "I also had my face lifted," she added. "Last year."

"Well," said Henry, rather at a loss. "Well for the time being it's worked out fine on the whole, hasn't it? I mean it's a jolly good effort, what?" He turned to the rest of the family as if asking for a round of applause or a vote of confidence. As he spoke Henry escorted her to an armchair while the others rearranged themselves so that they could examine her clearly.

"Yes," said Helga rather vaguely as she sat down. "They all have it done nowadays, so I thought I'd better too."

"I expect you needed it," said Anne cheerfully. "You must be getting on now."

"You look younger than ever," interrupted Henry. Helga seemed visibly pleased, though she was disconcerted that no-one had offered her anything to drink except tea.

"But tell me," Henry went on, "what held you up? Surely you should have reached the house long before now."

Helga told him about her damaged car.

"Faulty carburettor, I shouldn't wonder," muttered Henry.

"How awful!" exclaimed Anne happily. "What are you going to do?"

Helga shrugged her shoulders. She looked lost.

"Have you eaten?" Anne asked. "Because we've nothing in the whole rotten house."

"Oh yes, thank you, granny," answered Helga, calling the old woman by the name Kenneth had once used. "I had some sandwiches before I came up. I don't want to be a nuisance to anyone."

"Don't be a fathead – it's no nuisance," Henry reassured her. "We can easily put you up here for the night. Nothing simpler."

Mathilda looked hard and long at Henry. "No," she agreed without enthusiasm. "We can make up a bed for you easily enough."

"And you can be off tomorrow," Anne volunteered.

"I hadn't really thought about it," Helga spoke hesitatingly. ". . . It's awfully kind of you."

"Then it's settled," Henry declared with an air of finality.

Eustace had been listening intently to all this talk and was by now fairly confident of having established the identity of their visitor. She was not the vet's assistant as he had originally suspected. Elbowing his way past Anne and Mathilda, he approached so close to Helga that she became hypnotised by the two pieces of cotton wool reaching out from the old man's ears. "Now look here, Helga," he started. "I may have said one or two things in the past – that's as may be, and nine out of ten people would have done much the same – but now you've turned up trumps. There's no denying that and I don't mind admitting it. Of course it's not before time, but what I'm saying is that we all appreciate your kindness in specially travelling down here in . . . in our hour of need. It's something none of us will forget."

"Here, here," chimed in Henry.

Eustace placed a trembling hand on Helga's shoulders and gazed at her gratefully. There was a moment of absolute silence and Helga felt tears starting to her eyes at the thought of her sensitivity, her generosity. "I only did what I thought was right, granddaddy," she whispered. But if only, she thought, they would give her a drink.

"And now," said Eustace more cheerfully to the whole room, "let us have a small drink together to mark Helga's return and to wish for Smith's quick recovery."

In this atmosphere of optimism and goodwill even Mathilda, even Anne, consented to have a sip of cider. The glasses were circulated and for a moment everyone felt pleased with themselves.

It was better than nothing, reflected Helga. She allowed herself to be led over to Smith's divan and made a number of encouraging noises. She was still talking to the dog when the doorbell rang again. After a moment of paralysis, Helga was forgotten and everyone except Mathilda rushed into the hall. At last the vet had arrived.

The door was hastily opened and Mr Summers came in. Henry shoved his way forward. "Come now, ma," he said gently, "don't worry the vet." Then turning to Mr Summers he continued in his business voice: "Things appear to have taken a turn for the worse, I'm afraid. Appreciate it if you'd step over and take a look – appreciate it greatly." They began walking towards the dining room together while Henry continued pleasantly talking man to man. "Come over by car, did you? Got a Vauxhall myself. Expect you get around a bit – know the lie of the land."

As they entered, Mathilda who had been on her knees next to Smith, rose to her feet. "Oh, I'm so glad you have come," she almost sobbed. Wiping her hands convulsively on her skirt she continued with more restraint, "We've been frightfully worried. Everyone says he looks worse. I do hope you'll be able to do something."

The vet asked her one or two questions and then went across to the dog. Mathilda, twisting her handkerchief in her hands, crouched beside him, almost like another animal. Despite the suspense and her anxiety, the same heavy lethargy lay upon her and she felt numb with weakness.

Kneeling next to Smith the vet put his ear on the dog, which did not move. The rest of the family shuffled around embarrassed by their helplessness. Then the vet stood up and faced them. There was silence in the room.

Then in a quiet voice he spoke.

Chapter 25

A DOG'S LIFE

"I'm afraid," said Mr Summers, "your dog is dead. He must have died in the last minute or two in his sleep. It is the best way – quite painless. I could have done nothing for him had I arrived sooner."

"What did he say?" whispered Eustace.

Henry leaned right over and explained what the vet had said.

As soon as he had stood up, Mathilda had known it was all over. Yet there was something unreal about his words and a certain relief mingled with the sudden thrust of grief and desolation that passed through her. The strain, which for so many days had been steadily mounting within her, was finally broken. In a few brief seconds the tension was gone. But with this release, her tiredness also fell away and she was consumed with a burning restlessness. For a few moments she was unable to speak. There were no words. She bowed her head in dazed acceptance. Then the full horror presented itself. How would things be without Smith to occupy her? There was nothing. She was alone. It was all so pointless and unreasonable. Smith, who had been an essential part of her life, was gone – simply disappeared for ever. The public disasters of the world – the wars, earthquakes, political crises – were as nothing against this one reality. Her grief clutched at her heart, paining her physically. What was the point? What had been the use of anything she had done? Nothing made sense. There was no blame. There was an empty space. Nothing.

For a few seconds she must have lost consciousness. She could not remember the vet leaving the house. The next thing she heard was a lot of senseless whispering between Eustace and Henry. And somehow this was too much for her. She wanted to shout out loud, to run away. She hurried out of the room with a strange choking sound.

Miss Tooth followed her out.

Anne also headed towards the door, then hesitated, not knowing what to do or say.

Eustace moved in the direction of the vet. "Is there nothing to be done? Spare no expense."

Henry gently led the old man out of the room, followed by Anne and the vet. Helga was left alone. She shut the door, poured herself a large cider, gulped it down and then, with exaggerated slowness, walked out and joined the others in the hall. She wished she had returned home on the train. No-one was taking any notice of her, yet she could not leave. She sat down and watched the scene with sympathetic indifference.

The vet left quietly, almost unnoticed.

In a corner of the room, hunched up on a stool, sat Mathilda. Her eyes, wide and unblinking, seemed to focus on nothing. She rocked back and forward, her arms clasped around her body. Behind her, like a guardian, stood Miss Tooth in majestic silence. Anne walked to and fro, patting cushions, rearranging chairs now this way, now that, picking up ashtrays and putting them down, working herself into "a state". All the time she kept up a monotonous refrain: "Oh dear! Oh dear! Oh dearie me!"

Henry coughed and blew into his hands and then diffidently asked Mathilda whether she would like a drink to fortify her.

"No thank you very much," she answered, strangely gentle. "It's kind of you all the same."

"It's an awful shame, poor thing," remarked Helga. Then suddenly, overtaken by violent hiccups, she ran out to the kitchen to hold her breath and cautiously sip water from the back of a glass.

"Now look here, Mathilda," began Eustace, trying to console her. "Now look here, it's a damned shame as Helga said, and no mistake, but . . ."

He was interrupted by Henry. "Try not to let it get you down, old girl," he advised.

"Will you please permit me to finish what I was saying?" demanded Eustace, exasperated.

"Very well, pa," Henry replied with a long-suffering sigh. "What pearl of priceless wisdom are you about to let fall?"

There was a silence as Eustace struggled to remember what it was he had intended to say. "Now, Mathilda," he resumed lamely, "if there's anything you feel I can do, anything at all, mind you, just let me know." Then suddenly remembering what he had meant to say, he went on: "I know what. I'll get you another dog. I'll go and get one tomorrow if you like. A bigger and better one – if possible."

Little of what had been going on during these last minutes had reached Mathilda. None of her family, though they knew her so well, had lived with her so closely most of her life, and for whom she had renounced what had been best in that life, could now, in her moment of distress, reach out and touch her. For year after endless year they had passed and repassed one another on the same staircase, turned the same door handles, sat in the same chairs around the same tables, hearing the same voices mouthing the same formulas of words. The very tics and eccentricities that, so many years ago, had made them laugh, made them familiar and close, now irritated them beyond measure. As time had gone on they had become intimate strangers – strangers to themselves as well as to each other. They had constructed prisons for themselves from which they could not now escape. Mathilda saw them round her, heard their voices, but was alone.

Hearing Eustace's offer of another dog made her think. No,

she would never have another dog. That was certain. She no longer had the strength. She would rather exist as someone who was pretty well dead. The last ten years had brought her to her knees and made her irretrievably old before her time. Like the fine strands of a spider's web, a thousand tiny lines had spread across her face, making her look, even in sleep, engrained with worry. She did not flinch from this truth; she did not wholly regret the past – but she would not go through it again. She looked up at Eustace and spoke with a conviction that startled the old man: "No. I never want another dog. Never again!"

Besides, what had another dog to do with anything? She had wanted Smith and he had gone. That was the end of it. Yet, despite this loss, an irrepressible sense of lightness rose in her, as if a chain that tethered her had suddenly snapped, and she was free.

The world around Mathilda moved back into focus, the mingling of voices became clear and intelligible once more, the room took on colour. Whatever happened, she must not make an exhibition of herself. Life went on regardless of misfortunes and this itself offered her consolation. The past was dead and done with and no purpose was served in wasting one's time over it. She had known that already and must not forget it. She must pull herself together again as she had done after the war. If she started crying she knew she would not stop.

With a clumsy movement she stood up. Then, putting her

hand to her forehead, she began quietly lecturing herself.

"Mathilda Farquhar!"

"Yes!"

"This will never do!"

"No. It won't."

"Pull yourself together."

"Yes."

"And stop all this nonsense."

"I will!"

And she did. She seemed once more to gain possession of herself. Miss Tooth drew nearer to commiserate – but she was not needed. No-one, nothing, was needed.

Chapter 26

NIGHT

Self-consciously they hung around the house for the next two hours, feeling redundant.

Smith's body was covered with a red, white and blue rug, and left to rest until morning on the divan. After a while the family talked about other things: the price of food, the eccentricities of the weather. But their minds still circled round Smith and their words sounded irrelevant. Smith's death tracked them from room to room and up the stairs to their bedrooms.

Mathilda was the only one who appeared to have some other purpose. She immersed herself in a programme of work: speaking to the boiler, visiting the garage, washing up various unused plates and bowls, defrosting the refrigerator and dusting the hall. She hurried from one place to another, unable to remain still, unwilling to go to bed. By working so actively she hoped not so much to distract herself from thoughts of Smith's death as to overwhelm her grief through physical exercise, to undermine it with exhaustion. But by midnight she still seemed driven by nervous energy.

The others, under the abnormally prolonged strain of one another's company, unrelieved by any distraction from the television which in the circumstances, it was generally agreed, could not be put on "with any decency", were utterly spent. And so, shortly before midnight, imparting their last hushed words of solace to Mathilda, one by one they climbed the stairs to the chilliness of their beds.

Helga, having recovered from her hiccups, was the last to go, reaching the top of the stairs where Henry appeared, resplendent in a purple dressing gown. "Come along now, old girl," he chuckled, giving her a playful smack on her bottom. "You'd better be off to your couch or you'll never wake up tomorrow morning – if you're anything like you used to be. As for me, I'll have to be up at seven and in the office by nine. It's a dog's life – oh sorry, Mathilda."

Helga had not been allowed to make use of her son's empty bedroom since Anne insisted that the child would be returning soon that night on compassionate leave from the army. To bring the matter beyond argument she had double-locked the bedroom door. So Helga had been given Henry's room, while Henry himself was thrown a couple of old blankets and a pair of cushions to use as best he might on the floor of the landing. "Ma must be mad," he complained mildly, as he bent down to arrange his ramshackle bed. He frowned thoughtfully as

Helga kissed him goodnight, expressing the hope that he would not be too uncomfortable on her account. It would worry her, she volunteered, to think that he was not getting a proper night's rest before all that office work of his. She would lose sleep over it.

Henry felt his way awkwardly into the blankets. Sounds of Mathilda's housework floated up to him. What an impressive performance she'd given, he reflected. He felt damn proud of her. She had taken it almost like a man, you might say.

He shut his eyes. The darkness was filled with the vague forms of those cricketers whose job it was to entertain Henry during the night. A team of Belchers, it looked like this time, versus a team of old Harrises. Should be a close match.

Eustace was ready for bed. His false teeth leered from the glass of water on his bedside table; his bandages and supports lay uncomfortably over the back of his chair. He sat limply in his blue pyjamas on the edge of the bed.

Overriding his sorrow, the old man felt great pride in the way his sister had conducted herself before a stranger that evening. He would be sorry to lose the dog, though his thoughts centred on Mathilda. Everything during the next few weeks must be made as easy for her as possible. Anne would have to be watched like a hawk. Come to think of it, he'd better *have a word with her* in the morning.

One thing secretly troubled Eustace. Mathilda did not believe in God, and that made her misery all the more agonising. But then there was little religion circulating round the place these days. When he, Eustace, had been a child everyone was taught there was a God in Heaven who could see and hear everything you did and said. In those days you thought twice before doing or saying anything.

Conscious perhaps of the Deity's eyes upon him even at this late hour of the night, the old man knelt down on painfully creaking limbs and, covering his face with his hands, prayed out loud like a child that somehow all might eventually turn out for the best: "Oh Lord, who governest the unruly wills and affections of Thy people, make us to love the Thing which Thou commandest."

Anne had not started to undress and would not do so until she heard Mathilda come upstairs. She sat in front of her dressing table, listening and thinking.

Next to Mathilda herself, she thought that she would miss the dog most. Poor Smith! This'll Do would seem more of a dead place without him. He had such an aristocratic face too, such bearing. But then, she supposed, they would all (except Kenneth, thank God) "go" pretty soon now. Probably it was good riddance. She felt terribly tired these days and that must "mean" something. And, if that were not enough, she was shrinking, shrinking fast. At first it had given her quite a shock. As the months went by she had experienced more and more difficulty in seeing her whole face in the looking glass on her dressing table. For the last three or four months she had only been able to catch sight of her forehead. And even that, she very much feared, was beginning to go. She had to stand on tiptoe now, she had to jump. Soon she would vanish altogether.

Her eyesight was none too good either – not that there was much worth seeing these days. She would stare through her binoculars at the window for minutes on end, but to little avail. What a life it was! There must be something very wrong with the world. Only the other day Henry had been telling her how we were all descended from monkeys! The way things were, Anne would not be at all surprised if he were right for once. In any event, those fishes she had seen on the television the other day looked jolly healthy. They had a better time of it, she reckoned, than herself.

Whenever would Mathilda be coming up? She must be almost dead with fatigue. Normally Anne would have shouted down to her or blown a few blasts on her emergency whistle, but they were always telling her she was saying or doing the wrong thing – and she had no wish to make matters worse at such a time.

During the next half hour, she found some paper and a pencil and wrote young Kenneth a letter:

My darling Kenneth,

Just a line to ask how you are keeping. Fit I hope. Please excuse the pencil. Enclosed is a further 10/- – get yourself a nice lunch with it. I am taking the number of the note as there are so many dishonest people about today. Don't spend your pennies on Drink – it is the downfall of all the New Men. No news here at all. We never go out. Only wish things would improve, the price of everything is too awful. Poor Smith passed away on Tuesday after you left. Great Aunt Mat is most upset. It would be very kind to write her a few lines to say how sorry you are. Your mother arrived here but wasn't much use and goes back tomorrow morning. Do let me know if you want anything. I am sending on the hot-water bottle you left – the stone one for the army. Mrs Gaff goes away next week – don't know how we'll cope – will have to shut up the house if we're not lucky. I am having rather a heavy time of it for an old woman. Everybody seems on holiday, lucky brutes. They all send their love. I always said Smith was looking seedy – but no-one ever listens to what I say.

Fondest love

Granny

P.S. Shops will be shut on Sunday. So look out!

Having completed this task and read through the seven pages over which it was spread, Anne slipped the letter into a stamped and addressed envelope, and put on her coat and hat. It was half past twelve, time she reasoned for an expedition to the postbox. Not that she had any intention of really going out. Mathilda, she knew, would not let her. But it would give her an opportunity to see what she was up to. Taking a firm hold of her walking stick, she crept down to the hall. As she reached the last stair, a sound of singing was wafted through to her from the front garden. She stopped open-eyed. Then, before she had time to say "Jack Robinson", she heard a short double knock on the front door, setting her heart fluttering wildly.

So here they were at last – the cut-throats and burglars. But, on second thoughts, perhaps not. After all, burglars, she had read, seldom took the trouble to knock at doors. It was too early for carol singers, or too late, whichever way you chose to look at it. It must be someone else – probably the vet had come back for his money. How like a vet!

Emboldened by her sip of cider, she began opening the door.

Outside, under the lamp post, a car was parked. Over the gate, his face lifted to the stars, leaned the rather dishevelled form of an old soldier in uniform, his sword raised triumphantly in the air. He was singing with a weary gusto. It was obviously long past his bedtime. On the threshold itself, slumped forward on his luggage, sat the crumpled figure of Kenneth.

As she opened the door, her walking stick poised as if for duelling with the soldier at the gate, Kenneth looked up. His colour was high, his eyes shining.

"Well," he cried, flushed with success, "I made it!"

*

"Yes I know she's here," answered Kenneth, annoyed at being interrupted. "And then, as I was saying, we arrived at the mess and . . ."

It was five minutes later and having persuaded Colonel Humblemere to retreat to his home, Kenneth was telling his grandmother all that had happened.

"Do keep your voice down," whispered Anne. "You're shouting. You'll wake up everyone if you don't look out."

"Is that you, Kenneth?" asked Mathilda putting her head round the corner and looking at him.

Kenneth greeted her with unusual expansiveness. "Yes it's me alright. I'll tell you what happened. It's quite a story."

"Does he *know*?" Mathilda quietly asked Anne. But Kenneth, so talkative for the first time in his leave, was already chattering merrily away, telling his story.

"It happened to be Band Night up at the mess, and they'd invited the brigadier. I warned old Humblemere that we'd better call the whole thing off, but he wouldn't hear of it. He was an honorary member of the mess he said – something like that – and insisted on entering. About quarter of an hour after we'd arrived, they all rose from dinner and came into the main hall to listen to the regimental band for a few minutes before drifting into the anteroom for their brandy and coffee. The first to come in were Armstrong and the brigadier."

"Does he know about Smith?" repeated Mathilda.

"For a moment the four of us looked blankly at one another," Kenneth rambled on. "Then old Humblemere, without batting an eyelid, slapped Armstrong on the back and began speaking about his father."

"Do lower your voice," pleaded Anne.

"There was little enough that Armstrong could do but introduce the old boy to his guest the brigadier, though anyone could see he was frightfully put out. Luckily the brigadier and Humblemere got along like a house on fire. Armstrong tried to shut Humblemere up once or twice but without success. Then Humblemere explained to them both about Smith – so sorry to hear the bad news, Mathilda, by the way – telling him what a sporting dog he was and so on. And when he'd finished, the brigadier turned round and said rather loudly: 'Damn hard luck!' You hear that, Mathilda? His very words 'Damn hard luck!' After that it was plain sailing. Armstrong granted me forty-eight hours extension of my leave there and then. He seemed anxious that it should start and we should be off immediately. But Humblemere was enjoying himself and began to amuse the brigadier with some games they played out in India – travelling round the room without touching the floor and . . ."

"Your breath smells of drink," said Mathilda flatly. Kenneth's story about mess bands, brandy and brigadiers sounded highly implausible. The real explanation would have to wait until next day. All this pointless chatter irritated her unbearably. "I think it's time you went to bed now."

To her surprise Kenneth meekly obeyed. Anne clambered up the stairs after him, saw him step over the prostrate form of his father on the landing and begin to pull at his bedroom door handle.

"And who's mad now, I'd like to know?" murmured Anne as she passed the dim outline of Henry snoring gently on the floor under his blankets. She began rummaging in her pockets for the key.

Once inside his bedroom, Kenneth undressed quickly and got into bed. It had been a long day. Sleep spread through his limbs and a vision of Helen swam unsteadily before his eyes.

Suddenly the door rattled and Anne walked in. "Are you awake, Kenneth child?" He made no movement, but she went on: "Here's a letter I wrote you. It's stamped, so you'd better read it. Now don't stay up late. A growing boy needs his sleep."

Kenneth stirred. "That reminds me," he said sleepily. "I've still got a letter I wrote for my mother. Would you like to slip it under her door?"

Anne shook her head incredulously. "At this time of night? Don't be so silly, Kenneth. You can give it to her before she leaves tomorrow – that's the proper time. Now don't stay up all night reading. Good night."

And carefully placing her own letter on the eiderdown, she withdrew.

*

Two hours had passed since he'd hit the sack, and after the first forty winks he still could not drop off. The floor was damnably uncomfortable. The draft whistled about his ears and he was cold.

He thought of Helga in the next room, his room, warm, soft and comfortable in his bed. Extraordinary coming across her again like this. She had obviously been happy to see him. Scatterbrain though she might be, Henry had a tender spot for Helga. Always would have. She made him laugh – and she'd learnt to handle a car bloody well.

It was no good. He was too cold to sleep. Deciding to creep silently into Helga's room for a towel and a rug to put on his bed and cover himself, he got up, padded across the landing and quietly eased open her door. Then he stepped in and closed it behind him, this time less quietly. Helga turned towards him and smiled. "Hello," she whispered. "I couldn't sleep either."

Henry hovered at the centre of the room, his pyjamas clasped around him, his hair standing out straight on both side of his head like a lavatory brush. He was shivering. "It's pretty frigid out there, old girl," he murmured pathetically.

In the darkness he looked like an overgrown schoolboy at a late-night dormitory feast. Helga sat up and took pity on him. "It's warmer here," she said and wriggled across the bed.

"Thought I'd collect a few things for my couch," Henry went

on as if he had not heard her. He rubbed his moustache and began opening and closing various drawers in the chest of drawers, swearing faintly to himself as he rummaged through them.

Helga sighed in exasperation. "Henry!" she exclaimed.

"This old jersey should help too," he muttered. "I don't often wear it. But its time has come." Soon he had assembled quite a pile of odds and ends, but instead of leaving he sat on the floor, yoga-style, and started talking.

"Well, my dear, I must say it's been nice bumping into you like this. And tell me, how's old Poach?"

"Roach, Henry. Roach. Oh, Finsbury's alright."

""He won't mind you staying down here?"

"He won't even notice."

Henry frowned in the darkness, making the room seem darker still. Helga sighed. Was he going to sit there indefinitely, she wondered, cross-questioning her about her marriage? And this after having wakened her at two in the morning! Really, it was too bad! She would have no eyes at all by breakfast.

"How are you two getting along together, then?" Henry asked.

"Oh so-so, you know. Not too well, really."

"I'm sorry," murmured Henry. He got up and moved toward the edge of the bed. "Of course, as you can see, I'm on my own still. No-one else in mind at present. God knows where I go from here. I sometimes wonder whether we mightn't have made it together, you and me, if we'd stuck it out."

Helga thought of Henry's old bulging suit, the heels of his shoes, the short crinkled old school tie he wore, his depressing socks, his tobacco and those uneven braces. No, she thought, not really. But she said nothing.

"Yes," Henry went on. "I reckon with a bit of luck we might have made a go of things. But we were too young then."

Was it possible to be too young? Helga wondered.

For a while there was silence in the room. "It's impossible here, quite impossible," Henry muttered. "I'll have to go soon."

"Oh don't go," Helga said, misunderstanding him.

Henry shivered. "God's truth, it's bloody cold."

"But you're not going, are you?"

Henry shook his head thoughtfully. "I don't know what I'm going to do. Maybe I'll leave. Maybe I won't. It all depends."

Helga stretched out and took his hand. "It's warm enough in here," she said.

She could not sleep.

Although at last she had exhausted herself and felt sick with tiredness, Mathilda did not switch off her light. She sat bolt upright in her bed, her eiderdown littered with old film and fashion magazines. They were her only indulgence – or was it a weakness? Whatever it was, they remained the one glance at glamour she allowed herself, these lives which she could never lead herself. They lay across her bed, untouched and over-looked. He mind was focused on the past, on what might have been, what lay beyond these pictures. As the years passed by at This'll Do she had increasingly given in to daydreaming late at night. And tonight, for some reason, she found herself remembering Emilio and the wonderful times they had enjoyed long ago.

It was difficult to believe she had been the same person as she was now, difficult to believe any of it had happened at all. It had lasted hardly a year or two all told, which was not much in a lifetime. And yet it was everything. She could not help wondering what he was up to now, Emilio, where he lived and whether he ever thought of her – probably not.

Perhaps, after all, there had never been a chance of happi-ness. Who could tell? All she knew for certain was that the days they spent together were lit up in a way that had never entirely faded even after all these years. There had been nothing else like it. Along the few yards that led from the front door to the gate, she stepped with him into another world. And then it had to go wrong.

He had been a terrible rogue, of course, everyone had told her that. And Eustace had been perfectly right, just after she'd received that terrible letter from him, to tell her to forget the whole unhappy affair. Still, she *did* catch herself thinking about him late at night, and remembering the outrageous things they used to say and do. Silence didn't mean forgetfulness. She did not want to forget – or lose the pain. Whatever anyone cared to say about him, no-one could deny his personality, his charm, the way he made her laugh. She often wondered whether she'd really had so lucky a break as the family liked to make out. Anyway, he had given her what real happiness she'd ever had, and no-one else had been able to take his place afterwards – no, not with all his faults!

And just as life had gone on after he left, so now it would go on after Smith's death. The tears stood in her eyes as she thought of her dear old dog. His loss would be a great blow to her – she was only now beginning to realise how great. It would seem odd without him, so very quiet, so empty. If only things had been different. However, that was life, she supposed.

But even now she would not be alone. Her brother too would miss him; and Miss Tooth of course; and even Anne in her own funny way: indeed the whole family had been affected. He had been part of all their lives – and their lives would be diminished now. Hers certainly would be.

And so the days would go on. There was plenty to do. Tomorrow if it were fine she would paint the deck chairs, get some tiles for the roof, find the hose wherever Henry had hidden it, damn his eyes, in the garage. The garden would have to be washed thoroughly; the lawn brushed and combed too, since that crazy fool North had forgotten to do it last week. And there were the birds to think of. Oh, there was plenty to do alright. And if she worked hard and really set her mind to it, she might have time to clip the hedge at the front, which was in such an awful state at present, and make it look neat and respectable before the light faded in the sky and it was night.

And every day she would visit the end of the garden where the tangled undergrowth of roots and weeds and fallen branches lay thickest. For there, in a clearing and under a little mound of earth and smooth stones, and crowned with the blue china vase that now rested in the drawing room, she would bury Smith.

Three o'clock struck from the old church clock. Three notes, long and mournful, echoed hollowly through This'll Do. Mathilda reached out and switched off the light. In the darkness she heard the murmur of excited voices, Henry's and Helga's, from across the landing. Her loss suddenly cried out to her and the ache in her heart contracted with a painful twist in urgent need of consolation, of love.

She pressed her head deep into the pillow to blot out the sound. But the whispering persisted. It was everywhere: in the walls, the furniture, the bed itself – growing in volume, becoming hideously distorted, allowing her no peace. In despair she put both hands to her ears, relaxed, and lay still.

From the black sky above, rain began to patter delicately upon the roof, shivering and streaking down the windows, like tears.

POSTSCRIPT
Change and Delay

I read novels in my early years partly to escape anxiety and boredom. My parents had split up during the Second World War – and went on re-marrying afterwards. There perhaps lay the core of my anxiety. For the best part of twenty years my home was at Maidenhead, living with my paternal grand-parents. There increasingly lay the boredom. When I was in Maidenhead I wanted to be in London with my mother. But when I went to stay with my mother and her new Hungarian husband I longed for the familiarity of my grandparents' house. I did not know where I should be, what I wanted. I dreaded going to boarding school – and dreaded leaving it. Nothing made sense. I wished for security *and* excitement, the two in harmony together. I was uneasy when travelling during the holidays on brief visits to parts of France to see my French step-mother; or battling across the belligerent North Sea to Sweden visiting my mother's family. Everyone was kind to me in several languages yet so much was bewildering. No-one ill-treated me and I had no terrible enemies. Some of the boys at school envied me these journeys to foreign countries during those post-war years – and I pretended they were crammed with extraordinary adventures. In fact I seldom knew what was happening. This was the fact I attempted to embroider with fiction.

One solution to these problems was to read novels into which I could disappear and find happiness forgetting myself. I read Conan Doyle and H. G. Wells, then translations of French and Russian novelists, Balzac and Zola, Turgenev and Dostoevsky, also short stories by Chekhov and Maupassant. Here was an involvement without loss of security: no tedium, no alarm. It was probably this habit of acquiring a vicarious and imaginary extension of my life through reading novels that led me to try and write one myself. Unfortunately my fiction was eccentrically tied to my own experiences and reflected my family life as seen through a distorting mirror. I wrote and wrote without reaching any destination.

Recently I came across these writings belonging to my late teens and early twenties. I am appalled and impressed by the unrelenting quantity of words. My first attempt, in a dark-red hardcover exercise book, was spread over 262 pages of cramped handwriting like the tracks of a spider wandering along the narrow lines. My story (insofar as there was a story) appears to have the title *The Ones that Got Away*. To get away, of course, was what I wished to do. But where? The narrative of dire and discordant family life suddenly stops at the top of a page as if, after some eighty thousand words, I could endure no more.

I regained momentum by using a small manual typewriter. This time I turned out almost two hundred thousand words in single-spaced lettering over more than six hundred stubborn pages. Still the same subject, still no conclusion. But there was some improvement, some attempt to experiment. The first half is divided into five parts each written in the first person by a different member of the family. The second part is a third-person narrative, sometimes using the historic present. I think it was influenced by Joyce Cary whose novels I read and admired when I was nineteen or twenty. It is less forbidding, I think, than my previous draft. But I was not in control of what I was writing and could not steer the story towards a long-desired completion.

I must have written these two versions after I left school, while working as an articled clerk in a solicitor's office for eighteen months and after I completed my two years National Service in the army. How I kept going, and for exactly how long, I cannot now recall. But before leaving the army I began something different.

In the local library at Maidenhead I had come across the novels and biographies of Hugh Kingsmill. He had died in 1949 and was already a largely forgotten writer. I saw this as an opportunity rather than an obstacle as I set to work in various public libraries copying out the essays and reviews he had written that were not available in his books: first by hand, then using my new typewriter. It felt as if I were leading the life of a clerk in a Dickens novel. My plan was to hand this compilation to a publisher, presenting it as the bits and pieces of a jigsaw which, coming together as a revelatory picture, illustrated the contending forces of Will versus Imagination in human nature – all this to be nicely interpreted in a rather special introduction. Fortunately two of Kingsmill's friends, the novelist William Gerhardie and the biographer Hesketh Pearson, guided me away from this quixotic exercise and persuaded me to attempt a short Life of Kingsmill.

I found that I could escape from myself more readily when re-creating the life of someone else than when trying to re-invent my own life through fiction. *Hugh Kingsmill* was my first book to be published. I finished writing it in the late 1950s – and it was published by Martin Secker at the Unicorn Press in 1964, the intervening six or seven years being taken up finding a publisher. It might well never have been published if Kingsmill's friend Malcolm Muggeridge (then at the height of his television fame) had not written a lengthy and extravagantly generous introduction.

Kingsmill led me to my next biographical subject, Lytton Strachey. The poet James Michie, who was a senior editor at the publisher William Heinemann (one of the publishers to which I had sent my Kingsmill typescript), had gently explained to me that a first book by a wholly unknown writer about a largely forgotten author was not an obvious commercial proposition. But, he added, if I came up with a more practical subject he might offer me a modest contract. I suggested Lytton Strachey, about whom Kingsmill had written a perceptive critical essay, and this he accepted. I signed the contract on 5 October, 1961 and was given an advance of fifty pounds (twice what I had received for Kingsmill). Six years later the first volume of what had developed into a hefty two-volume biography was published by Heinemann. But how did I manage to survive for more than ten years without a job?

In a miserly fashion I had saved enough money during National Service to buy myself three or four months of civilian life. I also began to contribute a few reviews of books to magazines and newspapers after Hesketh Pearson had written letters recommending me to their literary editors. My family pitched in too: my father, mother and maternal grandmother giving me a small but vital allowance each month for a year and a half. Then, after completing the early chapters of my Strachey biography, I sent them off to an American publisher in New York and was given a rather more generous advance (840 dollars which was translated into 350 pounds). I also sent these sample chapters along with applications for grants to two American institutions, the Bollingen and the Saxton Memorial Fellowships, and was awarded both of them. Finally, Lytton Strachey's younger brother (Sigmund Freud's authorised translator James Strachey), who was his copyright holder and owner of a vast archive of family and Bloomsbury Group papers, handed me a cheque for 500 pounds so that I could afford to wait until the completion of my second volume before publishing my first. In one way and another I was extremely fortunate.

While I was still writing this book, emerging from the bath one morning as from a dream, I had a sudden perception of how I might quarry out a novella from all those multiple fading pages of fiction that had anchored me nowhere for so long (using up vast quantities of stationery – the very sound of the word said it all). It would be the best part of fifty thousand words long and cover the happenings of a family over twenty-four hours. I extracted this quickly and sent it for advice to William Gerhardie (to whom I had dedicated my *Hugh Kingsmill*). He responded by writing a preface which I placed on the top of my typescript and hurried off to London International, my brand-new literary agent. They forwarded everything to my publisher – and Heinemann offered me a contract with an advance on royalties that was ten times my advance in Britain for *Lytton Strachey*. But they did not want to bring out the novella until after the two volumes of my biography had been published.

In this interval I held close to me three batches of related documents. The first was Gerhardie's preface agreeably sprinkled with great names of the past from Gogol to the Caroline poets. His argument was subtle and, he conceded, not perhaps "the happiest way of inviting professional consideration".

A *Dog's Life* should not be read, he insisted, it must be reread. This might seem a difficult task for readers, but it was necessary because the subtext was of more imaginative significance than the text. Put another way, the narrative might, on first viewing, give the suspicion of being insufficiently empowered with vigorous action, deep plot and taut dramatic suspense. It was at this point of the argument that he introduced some great literary masters from the past none of whom specialised in page-turner thrillers. He went on to describe me as "a master of inconsequence" who had written his first novel "without euphoria, without a touch of sentimentality, with truth and humour, and submerged pity, so deep that you'd have to wear a diver's suit to find it . . . To ennui, he has been holding up the mirror to show boredom her own image . . . Mr Holroyd has written his *Purgatorio.*"

"The impact is devastating." This was one of Gerhardie's sentences that I would like to borrow and apply with equal generosity to his ingenious preface. There were nevertheless some passages in what he wrote that suddenly moved and encouraged me when I first read them despite the dense diver's suit I wore. "The little intermissions – the lie-down after lunch; the grandfather ever dozing off over his coffee and waking to drink it cold, or looking a little in the wrong direction when they all appear – like birds, suddenly disappear, and again appear – to see the grandson off; the television acting as a magnet to audible cross-purposes – these things and many like them . . . must be read to be enjoyed."

The claims in Gerhardie's preface may have imposed themselves on the influential editorial director at Heinemann, Roland Gant. He was a scholarly Scottish Francophile who had written several books himself and edited (among others) the novels of Anthony Powell and John Le Carré. He did not mention Gogol as Gerhardie had done but made an allusion to Chekhov and suggested that *A Dog's Life* might make "a very good play". I looked forward to this – perhaps initially a radio play, I thought – and still do look forward.

I believe the novel is to some extent an orchestration of gathering sounds, as if the characters are playing distinct musical instruments. It is also an attempt to attach special words and phrases to each member of the family, vocabularies that isolate and imprison them. The narrative makes use of a choreography mapping out everyone's movements through the house. Set some sixty years ago, it is almost a historical postwar novel. The language belongs to the past and carries the comedy; the tragedy is still with us in the circumstances of prolonged old age in bleak times. The family is caught in the aftermath of a war from which they have not fully recovered. They are confronted by what seems a hostile culture of raw, competitive finance, which they do not understand.

Roland Gant was aware that "biographers are sometimes indifferent novelists", but he asserted that I was "a real novelist, even allowing for some of this to be autobiographical in inspiration". He saw the book not as high tragedy, but a microcosm of the world in which what we have for lunch takes precedence over the strikes, earthquakes and wars which were little more than background noises heard on the wireless.

After so many years of writing-and-more-writing to no apparent purpose, these words of praise were deeply comforting. I remember slowly reading the final paragraph of this report, slowly drinking in each medicinal syllable – it surpassed anything I could reasonably have expected or imagined. At night, in bed, I had to get up and look at this last paragraph again. "Reading *A Dog's Life* gave me the same kind of sensation of being in the presence of real talent," Roland Gant had written, "as did the first production I ever saw of *The Three Sisters*, listening to *Under Milk Wood*, and reading *Mrs Dalloway* for the first time."

I copy these more-than-generous words now because they were to be rapidly confronted by overwhelming opposition. During the long wait for publication I had given the typescript to my father to read – and he was horrified by what I had written. His letters to me throb with pain and anger. For him the book was not a novel at all but a hostile caricature of the family. "You go out of your way to avoid any redeeming features in anyone's character," he wrote. ". . . Had you written down the name and address of the family you could hardly have done more to ensure that they were identified . . . The formula is evident. Take the weakest side of each character –

the skeleton in every cupboard & magnify these out of propor-
tion so as they appear to become the whole & not only part
of the picture. Please understand the whole family are together
in their dislike of this distorted picture you have drawn of
them."

The whole family had not in fact read the book, but my
father did speak to some of them. And what he said to them he
repeated to me. He accused me of having ignored my grandfather's great kindness during earlier years – a kindness from
which I had benefited. It was a mercy he was dead and could
never see what I had thought of him. My uncle too was spared
since apparently I had not made use of him. After the war he
had married a very rich woman and did not often go to Maidenhead, though he helped the family financially (something
my father was unable to do). The two brothers were not wholly
at ease with each other and my father took exception at my
borrowing his name, Kenneth, and fitting it on to the young
man who appeared to represent me in the book. "Could it be,"
my father enquired, "that he is the worldly & financial success
you so admire & therefore not to be offended?" He had not
spoken to my mother and "she may well have something to
say," he suggested. When I showed her the book, she remarked
that it was "a hoot", her special chapter being my parody of
pure, invented fiction. After learning this, my father omitted
her from the family's collective hostilities. "She apparently does
not mind what you write about her . . . she is as usual generous

at others' expense." His theory was that by changing her name with each marriage (he could not recall what her present name was) she had camouflaged herself and escaped from being identified.

To my surprise I was also let off from the accusation of libelling my father's Irish mother. "Strangely enough you seem to have dealt rather more gently with your grandmother. This I suppose is only to be expected considering she caused most of the misery. It was greatly due to her spendthrift habits that Father got into trouble with the Banks. Anyone who was unfortunate enough to be dependent to any degree on her, paid pretty dearly for that pleasure."

I tried to negotiate with my father, offering to rewrite some passages and use a pseudonym, but it seemed impossible for us to find a decent solution. One of our difficulties was that we kept colliding with each other in agonised agreement. "I don't drive like that!" he complained. "No-one does." "I know that's not how you drive," I replied. "I invented it. Would you like to add something?" "I certainly would not. I'm not writing your book for you." "What about subtracting something then?" I offered. "I'd like to subtract the whole book," my father concluded. We were both in a state of shock. His objections were most authentic, powerful and distressing when they focused on his sister (my aunt) and himself. He had not realised, he told me, how intensely I disliked them both. Changing a few passages was neither here nor there. Better to burn the whole wretched thing. "If it is a novel," he proposed, "why not introduce a few fictional characters & omit your aunt and myself?" But it was my inventions that particularly irritated him. He thought the publication of my book might actually kill my aunt. As for himself, presented as "a frustrated commercial traveller of tinned goods" and a hopeless failure ("I am well aware of it," he confessed), "I should have to give up my job. I am too old to stand that sort of humiliation."

I was nonplussed by this awful reaction. I had showed him a few pages from one of my previous narratives and though he had not been very enthusiastic nor had he shown any such hostility – possibly because he saw correctly that they would never be published. The characters in my final version were "comic but not laughable" Roland Gant had written and in my naivety I thought my father would be amused. He often said things about the family that were, it seemed to me, packed with greater aggression than anything I had written. But he did not say them outside the family. Though he wished I had taken a proper job as a solicitor or even in the army, he had invested in my attempt at writing mainly, I believe, in the hope that time would work it out of my system – though he might have been quite pleased, I think, if I had somehow succeeded. He had gone further, beginning to write novels himself once he knew I was writing one. His world had turned topsy-turvy after the war and he did not know where to find a steady income. In retrospect I believe he should have been an architect. As it was, he worked for a series of small building companies in Wales and England that eventually went out of business. If I could get something published, why shouldn't he have a go? He could certainly write – his letters to me are powerful proof of that. It was a gamble but what was there to lose? He wrote in the evenings, at weekends and between jobs – rather as I had done. After polishing off three or four business-like novels, he got so far as being taken on by a literary agent – but unfortunately no further. The publishers turned down his novels, while encouraging him to write more (to which, in a mood of rebellion and despair, he retaliated with a history of the world in verse). All of this may have added to his vulnerability. What neither of us realised was that first novels by writers over fifty are very difficult to place. I am somewhat in that position myself.

I used to see my father regularly in my twenties and on many Sundays we would drive down to Maidenhead for tea. There was no question of my holding him in contempt. Of course I had borrowed certain traits, gestures, tricks of speech and various mannerisms from members of the family but had fixed them onto characters with quite different careers and past lives. My novel was a study of ageing with the accent on old age, not a photograph of my family (let alone of myself). I said all this to my father – but now I am older I can more easily sympathise with how he felt. It is a matter of tone, as I see it, rather than of facts. Also I can say now what I could not say then. What I felt and thought about my family I have written in two volumes of non-fiction: *Basil Street Blues* and *Mosaic*. I did much research before writing those books and what happened to my paternal grandfather and particularly to my aunt was something close to high tragedy of which I had no knowledge before and has little or no place of my novel. Indeed I now know more than my father and even my aunt knew about some family secrets. When writing *A Dog's Life* my instinct told me that something emotionally dreadful had happened to my aunt. "Mathilda" (the person in my novel who is a sister not the daughter of the old man) transfers her love from human beings to animals. I cannot now read some of the pages towards the end of this book without tears.

"In the circumstances," my father concluded, "for my sister's sake and my own I must do everything to prevent this book being published anywhere till we are dead and I am prepared to take whatever steps that are necessary legal or otherwise." He reminded me that my book on Kingsmill had led to a lawsuit and my Life of Strachey to a legal objection as well as violent opposition from some of the Bloomsbury Group. "If your third [book] is going to involve you and your publisher in legal proceedings with the family, I don't think your reputation will benefit."

This was a strong case – and, acting as his barrister as it were, I can make it even stronger. It was true that Kingsmill's widow had threatened to take a case against me for libelling her on a couple of pages of my biography. She had promised to help me when I had met her in London shortly before she had gone to live in South Africa with her husband Tom Hopkinson who was to edit the magazine *Drum*. Once she had unpacked she would send me some correspondence and an unpublished manuscript of Kingsmill's last unfinished novel. But over the next eighteen months she did not send me anything. Instead she announced that she was writing a biography of him herself for the publisher Jonathan Cape. When, during my research, I met Jonathan Cape I asked him, striking what I thought was a professional note, about the proposed date of her publication. He told me that he knew nothing about such a book – information which I unwisely forwarded to Dorothy Hopkinson. She accused me of being "an angry young man" and we quarrelled.

In her excellent biography of William Gerhardie, Dido Davies reveals that Dorothy had been a girlfriend of Gerhardie's. He had introduced her to Kingsmill who fell in love and married her – after which she became the central figure of the two writers' growing enmity. I knew nothing of this. But as part of my research, I had talked with Gerhardie who, in Dido Davies's words, "used the opportunity to further his violent anti-Dorothy campaign". Hearing almost nothing from Dorothy, I accepted what Gerhardie told me of her coming under the influence of an Indian mystic who believed that the most perfect form of human expression was silence. Silence indeed was what I had received from her and silence, I wrote, appeared to be her most eloquent achievement. This was the mischievous page which, on legal advice, I rewrote. Both I and Dorothy, Dido Davies rightly concludes, "were unhappy with the book".

Gerhardie's preface to *A Dog's Life* was never published and never read by my father or, so far as I know, by Dido Davies. She believed that Gerhardie was investing in my early career in the hope that I would invest in the final years of his career. When in the 1970s a publisher brought out a ten-volume definitive edition of his books, I was invited to contribute ten individual prefaces to them. My experience in the writing of these introductory essays enables me to confirm Dido Davies's statement that he had grown "increasingly sensitive to criticism".

In labyrinthine prose, Gerhardie led me, like a Virgilian guide, through Purgatory, picking up and weaving in obscure and elaborate references, showing me what I should write and adding detailed instructions to "include the toothpaste story, leave out the Oxford scout, modify the girl with bandy legs, and change the first, third, fourth and eighth words of the second sentence and the seventh word of the fifth". His poetic improvements seemed to defeat what we both wanted which was to attract new readers to his novels. I struggled to introduce something more incisive and inviting. But when I persisted in keeping something of my own, he retaliated with a splendid thesaurus-inspired condemnation, calling me "a *smilingly* impenitent, pig-headed, bloody-minded, bigoted, intolerant, unyielding, inelastic, *hard,* inflexible, opinionated, fanatical, obsessed, pedantic, rook-ribbed, *unmoved,* persistent, incurable, irrepressible, intractable, impersuadable, cross-grained ruffian – no offence implied". My father might well have relished these words – though Julian Symons later wrote in the *Times Literary Supplement* that such qualities were what a writer needs. But when Gerhardie told me that he loved this definitive edition of his books which he looked forward to placing beside his bed and caressing like living objects in a Paradise Regained – adding that anything which jarred on these feelings would suffocate the happiness of his final years – I capitulated, taking out passages that worried him and coming up with a compromise with which we both could live. Might I have made a similar rescue operation over *A Dog's Life*? I doubt it, partly because I did not have the editorial skill to do so half a dozen years earlier.

My father's general criticism was that I had a blind spot about the reactions of people involved with my writings. "Your method of overcoming James Strachey's opposition to what you wrote in contradiction to his own views," he wrote, "was to alter anything that didn't matter & modify about 10% of the rest. You then fought a rear-guard action so that – finally – the agreed version did not greatly differ from the original." This is not what actually happened with my Life of Lytton Strachey, but it may reveal what my father feared might happen if we tried to reach a general agreement and I attempted to redraft the novel.

James Strachey had in fact devised a sophisticated arrangement for editing and improving my biography of his brother. When I completed the draft of my first volume I gave him the typescript and he began slowly working his way through it upstairs in his house near Marlow while I began work on my second volume downstairs. Eventually he went through every page of both volumes, sentence by sentence, criticising and correcting anything he thought was untrue or inaccurate. I learnt a great deal from this process – mainly of facts that were not recorded in the letters and diaries I had examined in the archive. Sometimes I disagreed with James's interpretation of these facts – then, as the author of the book, I was allowed to keep what I had written and James was permitted to add a devastating footnote below it. This, it seems to me, was a model arrangement between writer and copyright holder (I have switched to his first name in this paragraph because during these negotiations we became friends). He died shortly before my book was published but had read it all and given it his blessing.

There is little from which my father and I could have gained from this editorial exercise (he came once to collect me from the Stracheys' house and there was some analytical discussion beforehand between James and his wife Alix, the Freudian and the Kleinian, as to whether he should be offered a glass of sherry and what might be learnt from his manner of acceptance or refusal of it). My father was wrong about the working relationship between James Strachey and myself, and I think he was not altogether fair about my having such a blind spot as to the reactions of readers who appeared in my books. I had given the typescript of my novel to him and I was careful to send almost everyone who was alive the pages of my biography on which they appeared before the book was published so that I could modify what I had written.

But there was a significant minor character, Bernard Penrose, who was at the time seriously ill in hospital. Not being able to reach him, I gave him a false name and invented some superficial features to make identification of him difficult before revealing that he had had an affair in the 1920s with [Dora] Carrington who had become pregnant and had an abortion. Shortly after publication of my second volume in 1968 I received a letter from Penrose's solicitors challenging me as to whether "Piers Noxall" was in fact their client, Mr Penrose, now fully recovered from his illness. I could not deny this and the solicitor demanded that I print an apology and rewrite two pages of my book, giving Bernard Penrose his true name and deleting the brief love-affair and his responsibility for Carrington's abortion. This I did – though I could have challenged the solicitor and gone to court. For it was not Bernard Penrose himself who had insisted that I change what I had written, but his wife. Though the affair with Carrington had taken place before she had married him, he had never told her of this previous episode. Carrington had written about it in her as yet unpublished diary, though without clearly identifying Penrose who was to refer to this episode later when writing his unpublished autobiography in 1987 (which I read in 1993). "When I fell in love with another woman," he was to write, "Carrington was nearly forty. I found out only later that she had become pregnant and had an abortion. I wished that I had married her, but she said that she did not believe in having children." This passage would have hurt his wife far more than anything I had written. What I wrote was not judgmental, competitive or hostile. But she had been confronted by this affair for the first time (forty years after it took place) when reading my book. Was it true, she asked him, or untrue? And so as not to wound her needlessly he said it was untrue. Then, so as to avoid causing more trouble and discord, I rewrote the pages as the solicitor demanded – to the relief of my publisher as well as to Bernard Penrose himself. Unlike Dorothy Kingsmill, he had asked for no damages and was very helpful to me afterwards over my biography of Augustus John whose family he knew. Almost twenty years later on, in 1994 (that was almost seventy years after the affair had taken place and when Bernard Penrose was dead), I amended the pages and told the truth.

My father would have been right to point out that it seemed impossible for me to publish any book that did not lead to the threat of libel. And though I believe I was less blind to the sensitivities of living people involved in these books than he claimed, yet it is true to say that I did not appreciate how violent a commotion my Strachey biography would initially provoke. Among the bravest of those who, despite much anxiety and discomfort, allowed me to reveal their early homosexual love affairs was the artist Duncan Grant who went so far as to make a drawing of Strachey and give it to me for the jacket of my book. I saluted him and others who, having the courage in their old age to act on the Bloomsbury principles of absolute frankness, agreed to being shown, in the words of Frances Partridge, "naked and exposed". What they had done had been against the law and remained so until the Sexual Offences Act decriminalising homosexual acts between consenting adults over twenty-one was passed in 1967, a few months before my book was published. "Let those who feel tempted to dismiss the Bloomsbury group as a timid and self-regarding coterie," I later wrote, "ask themselves whether, had their own principles come to be tested in such an awkward practical fashion, they would have passed the test with such style and courage."

My main opponent, though I did not know it then, was David Garnett, whom James Strachey's widow Alix described as being full of "red-faced truculence and talk about libel actions". In her diary Frances Partridge records that he "violently entered the lists in favour of wholesale suppression". And it is he perhaps who best represents my father's view of the mischief my writings could produce. "He was 'on the whole in favour of truth in biography – but not at the expense of

211

the happiness of the living & their security'", writes Garnett's biographer Sarah Knights. "He maintained 'the rule should be roughly that physical details be omitted' and that biographers 'should not go into other people's love affairs'." There is an essential moral difference between writing of the living, who are vulnerable, and of the dead who may be kept in useful employment by telling us the truth once they cannot be damaged by such knowledge. For if we are merely fed with sentimental, false and protective stories about what people have done, we will be seriously misled as to the human condition, and morally cut adrift. There is also of course a difference between the imaginative flight of creative fiction and re-creative chronicle of non-fiction. In his late novel, *Ulterior Motives*, Garnett has a dig at me and also uses one of the characters to speak his own words: "What I would like to tell my friends – for I conceal nothing – I would frankly dislike to see in print." This is a wholly understandable position and one I tend to share. But I believe that David Garnett wanted more than this. If my biography was to be a signpost to the future then the private lives of the dead, and their erotic adventures when young, would eventually become public property. In David Garnett's case they were to be embarrassingly revealed in *Deceived with Kindness*, the autobiography of his wife, Angelica Garnett, who had believed she was Clive and Vanessa Bell's daughter but was actually the daughter of Vanessa Bell and Duncan Grant who, at the time of Angelica's birth, was having an affair with her future husband.

I feel sure that my father would have been sympathetic to David Garnett's ideal of keeping his private life for ever private. Of course we feel protective about those who have recently died as well as those who were close to us. Lady Ottoline Morrell's daughter, Julian Vinogradoff, after reading what Strachey, Virginia Woolf and others had written about her mother, took down the Bloomsbury pictures she had lent for the launch party of my book and left the walls at 15 Woburn Square, where the party was held, suddenly bare. It made little difference that Ottoline had been dead for thirty years. (Seen from a different standpoint a few years later, Ottoline came out far more sympathetically in my Life of Augustus John.) One of the most difficult decisions to make must have been for Paul Scott's family (including his wife and daughter) on learning from the typescript of Hilary Spurling's biography that he was bisexual. But they recognised the excellence of this biography, the tone of which was not judgmental, and did not censor it.

My father too was no censor of books. He enjoyed reading Boswell and Pepys. If writers wanted to make their own lives public, they should not be prevented from doing so. But since none of us live in solitary confinement and our lives embrace other people's lives, publication should preferably be left until most of our friends and contemporaries are safely dead. That was essentially my father's position and one that he would have wished me to follow in *A Dog's Life* – giving me the opportunity to look at the book again and, in my maturity perhaps, decide not to publish it.

It was Frances Partridge, I discovered, who came to my rescue over the publication of *Lytton Strachey*. In the debate among Bloomsbury Group friends, her arguments won the day. She had since 1939 been writing her diaries and would begin using them when publishing a number of autobiographical and biographical books in the late 1970s and then, from the mid-1980s onwards, bringing out several volumes of these diaries. They had been written without obvious plans to publish them and they were a considerable success, which added to the pleasure of her later years. I would like to think that her support for my biography helped to prepare for the publication of these diaries. But I have to add that in several unexpected ways the consequences of my book were to upset her – especially what she called its "vulgar serialisation" in the *Sunday Times* and the explosion of violent anti-Bloomsbury reviews by Geoffrey Grigson and others. I did not enjoy these reviews, but what shocked me were the number of letters I received accusing me of helping to spread cancer through the country and befouling our culture in such a way as to give support to our enemies in Soviet Russia. Had there been Facebook and Twitter in those days I believe I would have been buried in such stuff. But what particularly hurt Frances Partridge were the derogatory comments in the press about her husband Ralph Partridge (who had died in 1960) followed by the commiseration of friends, including Maynard Keynes's biographer Roy Harrod and his brother Geoffrey Keynes. The question she had to ask herself was: had she been misled in helping me with my biography? Some of her friends told her I was "odious", a "literary buccaneer" who took advantage of Bloomsbury's philosophy of freedom and who wrote "very badly" – all this I was later able to read in her diaries. But despite her agitation and uncertainties amid the swirl of aggression let loose by its publication, making her sometimes wish "the book had never been written", she remained loyal to it. "I find it absorbing," she wrote.

But there were other books that worried her, the chief one being, ironically, David Garnett's edition of Carrington's *Letters & Extracts from Her Diaries* which came out in the autumn of 1970. Frances Partridge noted in her diary that I gave it an "immensely long and very favourable" review in *The Times*. But for her "the past has been ruffled up and revived with all its conflicting and violent feelings," she wrote. "How strange that the sex life of a living person – Gerald [Brenan] – should be openly revealed to the world . . . had Carrington known when alive that her letters and diaries would be published, she 'would have been' amazed and horrified, I imagine."

Worse was to come when Ken Russell decided to make a film of the Carrington/Strachey story for the BBC with the beefy Oliver Reed playing Lytton. I immediately wrote and told

Alix Strachey, who then owned Lytton's copyrights, saying that it might help the sales of his books (and of my biography). She seemed unmoved one way or the other, but most of the people who had helped me with my biography were strongly against this proposal. "I feel there is a valid distinction between a biography and the televised dramatisation of a life," Carrington's brother Noel wrote to the BBC. Frances Partridge agreed with him and went into battle. "I feel amazed," she wrote, "at the extraordinary way I am venturing to try and stop their plans." But stop them she did, having got a promise from David Attenborough that the film would not go ahead without her consent.

But she was not successful with a play for the theatre called *Bloomsbury* by Peter Luke. As Carrington's copyright holder she got hold of Luke's agent, read the script and contacted a lawyer. She very much disliked what she read but came up against a legal quandary: the fewer passages that were directly quoted or closely paraphrased from Carrington's writings the less power she had as copyright holder to prevent their use. Thoroughly inauthentic speeches were beyond her reach. In the end she gave up the battle and the play was staged at the Phoenix Theatre in London. Daniel Massey was a memorable high-pitched Strachey and Penelope Wilton a wonderful boyish Carrington in what was almost a fictional recreation of what happened. The play itself lasted five weeks in the West End – and not long afterwards Massey and Wilton married.

There was more "mischief", as my father would have called it, emanating from my book during the '70s: first an exhibition of Carrington's pictures in the West End of London opened by Lord Eccles with a highly objectionable speech claiming that Carrington was an amateur artist who took up painting in preference to having a child; then a reading from Carrington's letters on the radio by Jill Bennett whose husband, John Osborne, approached me wanting to make a film of Lytton Strachey's life (he later used elements from the story, Strachey becoming a model for the dying biographer in *Watch It Come Down*); there were also numerous books on Bloomsbury, not all of them welcome to Frances; and the setting-up by G. E. Moore's biographer Paul Levy and myself of a charity funded through Alix Strachey's will and using money after her death from the sale of the Strachey archive to the British Library (as well as from the remaining years of Lytton Strachey's royalties) to create a computer location index of manuscripts and list of copyright holders – which Frances Partridge thought to be at best idealistic and at worst a bid for power. "I cannot help thinking of him [Paul Levy] and Michael as vultures," she wrote. Neither Paul nor I made any money from these schemes and fortunately the Strachey Trust projects, under the director-ship of David Sutton at the University of Reading, have been of lasting value and genuine use to scholars.

But the most disturbing of all these incursions was Christo-pher Hampton's film *Carrington*. In her authoritative biography of Frances Partridge, Anne Chisholm quotes a letter I wrote to Frances which I had forgotten – and which I wish my father could have read. "There have been a considerable number of people over the years who've thought they wanted to write a play round the book," I wrote. "I've stuck to the formula we agreed after the Russell fiasco . . . that is, I would head off any people who I thought were either not serious and talented or whose approach seemed to me very wrong. If there was a real writer who wanted to do something with my book, I would explain all the difficulties and complications but not oppose him or her personally. If [s]he actually produced something after all this, I would see that it was sent to you and that you were involved in whichever way you decided was best. In other words I would not indulge my own financial interests at the expense of your emotional interests; but I would not scotch all hope of some financial reward."

Frances agreed to this arrangement. She was to like the Christopher Hampton film script far more than Peter Luke's play. But she hated the idea of a film far more than a play, though she did not seem particularly perturbed by the fact that there would be an actress (it turned out to be Alex Kingston) in a small part playing her. She suspected I might have made some money from Peter Luke's play and possibly from John Osborne (neither was true) and she knew that I was willing to sell the dramatic rights in my book to whoever made Christopher's film. I took him to meet Frances and on the surface we got on well. But she was now in her mid-to-late seventies and had had enough of these continual disturbances. "I thought: you are not as charming as you thought you were," she wrote of us in her diary. ". . . after they had left I felt two crows had been pecking at my carcase . . . I wish they would wait till we're dead, even though our longevity may be a nuisance to them." My father would have understood her. In fact there would be a wait of some twenty years while *Carrington* passed from film company to film company and through a minimum of eight or nine drafts. By the time final cuts were made after the completion of the film, Frances was in her mid-nineties. Emma Thompson was a heart-breaking Carrington, Jonathan Pryce an authentic Strachey (his dancing was spectacularly good) and the film won three awards at the Cannes Film Festival.

Frances Partridge's belief in my biography, after the many agitations it had aroused and the criticisms levelled at her for supporting me, was remarkable. But there stood a fundamental difficulty between us. We did not agree, and never had, about her husband Ralph Partridge. It must seem incredible that I could maintain my view about someone I had never met in opposition to that of his wife. It was as if I were sinking back into a family turmoil like that which had overwhelmed my novel.

Logically it was quite easy to reconcile our differences. I believed that Ralph, the brave army officer who was awarded the Military Cross and Bar in the First World War, was a very different person from the older Ralph who was a pacifist during the Hitler war. He had met Carrington and Strachey in the summer of 1918 and worked as an assistant for Leonard and Virginia Woolf's Hogarth Press at the beginning of the '20s. His infiltration into Bloomsbury and especially his friendship with Strachey had made a great change in him by the time he first got to know Frances after the summer of 1923. Frances blamed Gerald Brenan for misleading me about Ralph – but Brenan had become a close friend of his in 1915 and knew someone almost unrecognisable to Frances. The trouble was that people who read my book and were looking for dramatic contrast used the early Ralph ("the Village Don Juan," Virginia Woolf called him, "... [who] behaves like a bull in a garden") at the expense of the more interesting, complex and mature man who, after Carrington's suicide, was to marry Frances in 1933. When I sent her the typescript of my book in the mid 1960s, she made a few small adjustments to the text and was content with what I had written – but then became understandably discontented by what some reviewers and readers thought of Ralph. In the early 1990s I prepared a greatly revised one-volume version of my biography. Again I sent the typescript to Frances – and she made hardly any alterations. When the new book was published in 1994 she reviewed it handsomely in *The Spectator*. We lived by then in more liberal times and few readers were deeply shocked by what I had written about homosexuality. But we had to come through stormy times to reach such tolerance. And all of us had made some contribution to this change.

David Garnett had argued that my book would "harden people's reaction against homosexuality" and that it would have been better to write in general terms of "great friendship rather than love". I challenged this belief. "If Lytton's homosexual loves were treated not slyly or sensationally," I wrote to him, "but with openness and truth, using what was emotionally significant just as one would in describing a heterosexual love, then this would have the effect of increasing tolerance."

Garnett's *Carrington: Letters & Extracts from Her Diaries* was part of this increasing tolerance. It is true that he edited himself out of these writings, omitting passages with disobliging or complex references to his sex life. Some of Carrington's "jokes about buggery" also gave him trouble, but the number of words he cut was partly influenced by his publisher Michael Howard. Garnett was concerned about offending living people, some of whom he knew. Nevertheless the book, even with these omissions, could not easily have been published before the mid-1960s. There were expectations that his Carrington volume would be a corrective to my biography. Garnett had accused Strachey of not having encouraged Carrington's painting and drawing, but he began the extracts from her letters after she had left the Slade School of Art – leaving this period of her life to Ronald Blythe's *First Friends* which was published, with the encouragement of John Nash, in 1997.

Shortly before his death in 1981, having heard a documentary I wrote on Lytton Strachey for BBC radio, David Garnett was to send me a very generous letter telling me how much he enjoyed it. As to my biography, his only complaints were that I had been wrong about Lytton's attitude to his family and inaccurate about the Apostles at Cambridge. I believe that by now he had accepted as inevitable the change that had come over biography during the previous fifteen years. His three entertaining volumes of autobiography, published in the 1950s and the beginning of the 1960s, show him as a happy and attractive heterosexual lover with no bisexual diversity. He did not mention in his letter my treatment of homosexuality which had initially so angered and shocked him. "Discretion is not the better part of biography," Lytton Strachey had written. I took this as my passport to the future when there would be little moral distinction between homosexuality and heterosexuality. I know that this is what James Strachey wanted and I was embarrassingly delighted when, after publication of my book, I received invitations to what I discovered were all-male dinners. I felt, in a small degree, as if I were the equivalent of John Howard Griffin, the white Texan who, with a doctor's assistance, artificially dyed his skin, turning himself into a black man at a crucial period of the civil rights movement and travelling through some of the most racially separated states of America to show readers of his book *Black Like Me* what black people were having to endure.

None of my later books were seriously threatened by the law. When I published my Life of Augustus John in the mid-1970s readers and reviewers generally took the view that his sexual adventures were like those of Henry Fielding's *Tom Jones* (in which, Fielding wrote, "the provision . . . we have made here is no other than Human Nature"). In short I had written a heterosexual comedy. But when I brought out a revised edition of the book over twenty years later, I found that the moral climate of the country was changing and that I was now the author of a cautionary tale. Towards the end of my book I described Augustus John in his early eighties holding a torch and wearing his beret one night as he fumbled his way upstairs and heaved himself into the bedroom of one of his illegitimate daughters (then in her late thirties):

> "Thought you might be cold," he gasped, and ripped off her bedclothes. He was panting dreadfully, waving the torch around. He lay down on the bed; she put her arms round him; and he grew calmer. "Can't seem to do it now," he apologised. "I don't know." After a little time she took him down, tucked him up, and returned to her room. It was probably his last midnight expedition.

I had been told this by the daughter herself, and although the family was not altogether pleased to read the episode, it did not surprise them and they did not challenge the truth of what I had written. Readers of the first edition had generally thought of John, with his crew of jokers and gypsies, as a naturally gifted tragi-comic hero and saw this event as being in the nature of Mr Pickwick's night-time misadventures at the Great White Horse Inn. By the mid-1990s some readers took a more puritanical view of John. It was as if a coin had been spun into the air and come down either on the side of greater understanding or of stricter disapproval.

What I had been attempting to do in my biographies was sympathetically described in a British Council brochure by Richard Holmes. These books (and he included my Life of Bernard Shaw) pursue "the underlying tragi-comedy of liberal aspiration into a darkening twentieth century," he wrote.". . . They reconstruct and re-animate a tradition of imaginative dissent, the vision of an alternative liberal civilisation, which is more like a manifesto for the future."

During the last dark years of the twentieth century and in the bleak early years of the twenty-first, the popular culture of the country was dramatically changing. It appeared as if we regretted some of the freedoms we had won and wished to punish, in the name of justice, anyone who had taken too great an advantage of them. Section 28 of the Local Government Act in 1988 seemed to support this. The Act stated that a local authority "shall not intentionally promote homosexuality or publish material with the intention of promoting homosexuality" or "promote the teaching in any maintained school of the acceptability of homosexuality as a pretended family relationship". Though this led to a number of lesbian, gay and bisexual support groups in schools being closed down, the Act may have been introduced by the fear of Aids after it first struck the country. The legislation was withdrawn in 2003 – after which gay partnerships have gained the respectability of legal status.

I remember thinking after the Second World War that no-one during my lifetime would go to war again. Surely we had had enough. How wrong I was! It is this atmosphere of violence, sometimes fuelled by the eccentricities of religion, that has most surprised me. Our violence wears the cloak of aggressive morality and also presents itself to us each evening as entertainment – often from America with its worship of the gun. In 1950 the word aggression was used as a pejorative term: now an aggressive marketing policy is what we admire as we compete with one another like schoolboys. We have replaced blood snobbery with celebrity snobbery and the media is crammed to bursting point with sport, crime, sex, money – and more sport. The amiable days of our endearing, comic athlete "Eddie the Eagle" have long gone and we now solemnly invest in the nation's sport as, to our incredulity and disgust, totalitarian regimes used to do.

We are encouraged to remain adolescents all our lives: we call our soldiers "kids", our lovers "baby", our mothers one-syllable "mums". Music and literature have faded from our education system, while science is held up as a money-making discipline. The single purpose of going to university is to "make money" as if we live in a mint. Money is no longer a means to an end – it is an end in itself. We ingeniously borrow from the future and, when we reach that future, find it barren. Fear and anxiety seem to thrive on carbon dioxide: we live in fear of failure, fear of change, fear of other people. We barricade ourselves in: our new houses, with their tiny windows which only the Artful Dodger could get through, resemble small prisons. We believe that greater punishments will protect us and that errors of the past deserve retrospective revenge. The dead are guilty until proved innocent. Give us a democratic referendum and we will happily vote for the reintroduction of corporal and capital punishments.

Are we travelling backwards and risking an evolutionary disaster preceded by an environmental one? Or is our culture part of a natural ebb and flow? That it might be the former was what Bernard Shaw feared when, in his mid-nineties, he made a will creating a charitable trust for the creation of a phonetic alphabet – a writer's basic weapon, reputed to be "more power-ful than the sword". "His expressed purpose was not his real purpose; he did not want to save ink and paper, help the child and favour the foreigner," wrote Jacques Barzun. "What did he want to do? Simply to get rid of the past, to give a part of mankind a fresh start by isolating it from its own history and from the ancestral bad habits of the other nations." There was nothing phoney about Shaw's alphabet. It would involve less cumbersome grammar and tiresome penmanship. In practical terms it would help to break down social barriers and reduce the number of semi-literate people in the population as well as international misunderstandings. It was a metaphor for the re-invention of our future. He invited the English to embrace a better word notation, to use one symbol for each sound, bringing together what we saw with what we heard. The poetry of this alphabet lay in its algebra and arithmetic, in the encoding of these symbols and ciphers and the magical choreography of its text. Put this phonetic alphabet next to the traditional alphabet and let us see which was fitter to survive. That was his challenge. At the very least this phonetic experiment would gain us more time – and with more time we might avoid an evolutionary disaster. To many people's surprise, Britain was to change its coinage, its measurements for distances and weights and also its readings of the temperature. But not its lettering.

When I write of our present predicament, it is not Shaw's voice I hear so much as my father's. He likened the late twentieth century to the last days of the Roman Empire with its endless gladiatorial contests. The banker barbarians were at the gate. But I did not think of writing a state-of-the-nation novel even in miniature form. All I was qualified to write about was the bereft and shrinking world occupied by the elderly.

It was my father's promise to take legal action against the

publication of A *Dog's Life* that shocked my publisher; it was the intensity of his grief and anger that shocked me. So, to my publisher's relief, I withdrew the book and handed back my advance.

But I had also sent a copy to my American publisher, Holt, Rinehart and Winston, who offered me an advance of three thousand dollars. I explained my father's strong objections to Tom Wallace, my editor in New York. In the summer of 1968, he sent the typescript to a Park Avenue lawyer. This lawyer advised us that there was a potential libel of my mother in the book. She might think herself placed in a "compromising situation" with several gentlemen callers and all-too-brief husbands one of whom was "engaged in industrial agriculture". Was there such a town-and-country gentleman in her life? The answer was no. As for my father, he might win a case in court if he were attached to his father's "corned beef business in Canada", had been "involved in celluloid" and seen his business recently merged. Was it true, the lawyer also wanted to know, that my father drove a distance of some twenty miles each day from where he lived with his parents to the office? Had he, as a schoolboy, attended Repton where pupils were apparently taught to speak French when discussing family matters in front of children and servants? Finally, was he a determined and erratic smoker of pipes? None of this was remotely true – though my father had for a short time in the past, I believe, smoked a pipe. At the end of his four-page report, the lawyer concluded: "We do not believe that, if the work were published in the United States, there would be substantial risk that a reader would be likely to identify Henry with Mr Holroyd. The Holroyd family simply isn't that well known in this country."

Tom Wallace told me that this last paragraph seemed to be "the real point". There would be little danger of being brought to court in America and almost no likelihood of personal damage being inflicted on my family in Britain. So I decided to go ahead and *A Dog's Life* was published in the United States in the spring of 1969. Although described as being "as exiguous a portrait of eccentricity as Holroyd's biography of Lytton Strachey", the reviews were generally more friendly than I expected – possibly encouraged by the reviewers' relief at being confronted by a book so much shorter than my previous one. *Publishers' Weekly* called it "a perfect delight" and described it as having a "populace of gentle eccentrics as hilarious as they are endearing". Readers of *The Atlantic* were told I had written a *jeu d'esprit* that provided "effortless entertainment". Only in less well known journals was there something closer to what I had tried to communicate. Under the headline "The Sorrows of Silence", the *Wichita Falls Times* reviewer warned readers that, though readable and thought-provoking, *A Dog's Life* was "a sharp comment on a wide-spread problem of today's society – self-imposed isolation or inability to communicate".

My aunt never heard of this novel and my father only became aware of its publication much later – mainly through someone who, as is so often the way, had read the reviews though not the book. By that time his anger had abated and he was encircled by financial worries which I was able to alleviate a little with my American advance for *A Dog's Life*. In the early 1970s, the advance on royalties having been earned, I made special arrangements with Tom Wallace to put the book out of print early and have the rights reverted to me – and with that the story was over. Almost over: since my father, who believed in Polonius's advice to his son "neither a borrower nor a lender be", made some poignant and ingenious attempts to pay me back (in all senses of that phrase).

My original plan had been to write books of fiction and non-fiction alternately – rather like the travel writer and novelist Colin Thubron who was also published by Heinemann where the receptionist always called him Michael and me Colin (later we took this up and solemnly swopped our first names once a year).

I was very fortunate to be writing biographies during the last thirty or forty years of the century – a period largely belonging to the work of the two Richards (Richard Ellmann's *James Joyce* and Richard Holmes's *Coleridge*). It seemed a stimulating period in which biography was expanding the possibilities of its form. I was one of the practitioners who benefited from (and was credited with) the bringing about of a quiet revolution which saw biography emerge as, it was said, "a rival to the novel".

In fact I do not think the novel and biography are rivals so much as catalysts. They are two branches of our past and present literature which are better described as creative and re-creative writing than fiction and non-fiction. Those over-simple and old-fashioned library terms separate them and imply that novelists and playwrights are confined to fantasy, invention and entertainment (as we imagine children's writers to be) while the business of biographers and historians is to assemble solid facts in chronological order (like soldiers on parade) for the special use of scholars who are collectively in charge of our country's annals. But there has always been a trade between the novelist of contemporary life and the biographer of past times, the one asking "Where are we now?" and the other asking "How did we get here?" The play-wright and novelist, from Shakespeare to Hilary Mantel, have found stimulus for their work within books by historians and biographers.

There were no university training courses for writing when I began my first wearisome attempts at a novel. But the sheer practice of writing, the marathon of penning so many words week after month after year, and then the baleful reading of it all, was a rough-and-ready, hit-or-miss process of training. And my wish to write fiction, followed by my Life of Hugh Kingsmill who was a novelist as well as a critic and biographer, helped me, I believe, towards becoming a writer of lives in whatever medium.

What I discovered was that biographers are not narrowly restricted to proven facts. They must take into account their subjects' fantasies, lies, dreams, delusions and contradictions, the wayward public reputations and the pattern of misleading memories. They must not invent but they may speculate. They may use parody as a form of criticism and plant direct quotations from diaries and letters in the page to change the focus of a narrative and give it the immediacy a novelist achieves with dialogue. And then they must find what their subjects' enemies have to say and use this opposition to give tension and drama to the story. They are telling a story, as well as exploring human nature. So they must present arresting contents on the page that is before the reader and at the same time make that reader wish to turn the page and find out, as the past is brought into the present, what happens next. Biographies usually end with the inevitable tragedy of death – the death of someone the writer has never met but in whose company he or she has lived, holding her letters, reading his diaries, being in communication it seems with the dead, trying to bring them back to life upon the page. As for myself, I long to finish my biographies and be rid of the haunting anxiety that I will never find a path through the puzzle of a life. But when I do reach the end, my occupation's gone and I am left in grief. It is as necessary for a biographer as for a novelist or playwright to have access to a sense of humour which may be used even in a tragedy. But there is no necessity for a biography to end with death. It may be a story told backwards or a story confined to the most creative part of the subject's life.

I read as many novels as I read biographies – I always have. But I did not know when I wrote *A Dog's Life* that, by the beginning of this century, there would be academic courses in first novels and one or two small publishing houses specialising in them. A number of these first novels (such as Philip Pullman's *The Haunted Storm* and John Banville's *Nightspawn*) were brought out by talented unknown writers who later became well-known successful novelists. For technical or perhaps autobiographical reasons these books became embarrassing to their authors, who have not allowed reprints. Other first novels (including Rainer Maria Rilke's *The Notebooks of Malte Laurids Brigge*) were written by those who went on to specialise in different forms of literature. And then of course there are one or two first novels which were also last novels, such as Sylvia Plath's *The Bell Jar* which has established itself as a singular classic.

The novelist Nicholas Royale, who is a Senior Lecturer in Creative Writing at Manchester Metropolitan University, teaches a course on first novels (his own *First Novel* being, I calculate, the sixth or seventh novel by him to be published). In *The Guardian* recently he wrote: "First novels are special. They represent the first thing a writer wants to say about the world. They are often believed to be heavily autobiographical. Many first novels will of course not be first novels at all, but may represent the fourth, fifth or fifteenth time an author has sat down to write a novel." All this I can recognise easily enough. There is also a tradition, I learnt (and I am anxious to pass this on), that first novels are "a distinct genre" treated gently by reviewers. But in this article there was no case of a writer turning from fiction to what is called non-fiction.

Literary biography has not been much valued at universities during the last forty years. In the late 1960s Roland Barthes published "The Death of the Author" and announced that literature should be released from the tyranny of individual experience. From then on the text belonged democratically to readers who employed academics – professors and doctors of letters – as their professional guides and interpreters. Literary biography had little or no place in this arrangement, partly because the genre itself did not deal primarily with literary theory but tended to reduce imaginative work to the remorseless trivialities of writers' lives – what they ate for breakfast, where they spent the night. There was, it seemed, a struggle for authority over the reader, over the writer's text. I remember hearing a talk by the novelist Ali Smith who made a passionate attack on the literary biographer's insistence that an auto-biographical impulse lay behind the process of creative writing. Nevertheless, she concluded, it was true that it did (though truth can be exploited in plenty of misleading and superficial ways). My own belief is that writers' lives lie invisibly between the lines of writing and some knowledge of these unseen lives can enrich the narrative.

Biography has partly been replaced in academe by Life Writing, which belongs more to social history. The subject whose name may appear on the title page represents a category of people who have been under-privileged and ill-treated in the past, but who can be given retrospective justice in the book. It is a form of group biography written with a moral purpose.

Since none of us live in a vacuum, all biographies are to some degree group lives. When I wrote about Lytton Strachey I was describing the Bloomsbury Group; with my Life of Bernard Shaw I fell into the company of Fabians. My one biography that was actually classified as a group biography has been *A Strange Eventful History* which told the stories of two families over a couple of generations covering more than a hundred years.

Most novels too of course are group affairs – even *A Dog's Life* which focused on the lives of five people over twenty-four hours. If I publish it now, almost sixty years since it was originally written (and more than forty years after its publication in America), I can hurt no-one anymore and damage no-one's reputation – except my own.

And having decided to publish should I edit it, try to make it a better book for people to read (or accept suggestions from an in-house editor to that end)? Or should I leave it exactly as my father read it (minus a few literals)? To print the book as it was, the history of which I have been describing, seems in this context authentic. I have largely revised my biographies, but that was because there was much new archival material available which paradoxically enabled me to shorten them. Then again, "there is a chagrin of authors", as William Gerhardie wrote, "not shared or realised by readers and ignored by librarians, a pious wish, for ever thwarted, to withdraw from circulation earlier, unpurified, inferior texts and versions of his books, to be replaced by a revised edition, and frustrate the nonsense of first editions."

So which is the better option? Finally I decided on a compromise: tightening and tidying up parts of the narrative by using, for example, one adjective in place of two or three (and eliminating those on other pages), changing several chapter headings and removing some obvious explanations and repetitions (though keeping others to mark the pattern of the writing) – and then submitting the book to a few house style changes. None of this editorial business has changed the nature of the characters or their attitude to one another and I believe that such changes, had they been offered to my father, would not in any way have altered his verdict. The first edition was dedicated to my mother and this I have removed for no reason other than that she is long dead now. That this present edition is somewhat shorter than what my father read might have struck him as a move in the right direction – but it is no more than a few paces instead of a full lap of the track he wished to see ending up at the beginning with an empty page.

I have had various invitations and opportunities to renew this novel, but I did not get round to rereading it until Christmas 2012. And when I did read it, some fifty years after writing the first draft, I found there was a shock waiting for me: the shock of recognition. Many of the traits in my family that I so keenly observed in my teens and fitted here and there on to my characters, are my traits now. I possess them. They belong to me. Whatever genre I was employing – satire, farce or parody; surrealism, tragi-comedy or scene individable – bringing this novel back into print may be seen as a brave, possibly foolhardy, exercise. Some of the family's objections have, up to a point, become my objections too. I regard this as is a subtle act of justice. It is the saddest comedy I have written.

MICHAEL HOLROYD was born in 1935. He was educated at Eton and completed his education in public libraries. His biographies of Lytton Strachey, Augustus John, Bernard Shaw and Ellen Terry established him as one of the most influential biographers of modern times. He was awarded a CBE in 1989 and knighted in 2007. He lives in London.